Craving the Love of a F**k Boy 2

A novel by Lady Lissa

Recap from book one

Zach

I would be the first to admit that me and Noelle's relationship took off kind of fast. After that first date, she and I had been spending an abundance of time together, especially now that she was on summer break from school. She was such an amazing woman and after she told me about her last relationship, all I wanted was to make things better for her. Her self-esteem was shot so low that I had to work overtime to get her to see just how beautiful she really was.

She and I exercised on a regular basis because she was uncomfortable with her weight. But make no mistake about it, I told her that I didn't care about her weight. My parents taught me early in life to love people for who they were on the inside and they will shine on the outside. That was how I lived my life. I didn't judge anyone and praised Noelle for remaining strong through everything she went through with that other nigga.

The question I kept replaying in my mind was why was she on her way to the hospital? Was she okay? Was it serious? I was already on the road when I got the call, so instead of going to my original location, I just headed to the hospital to check on Noelle. I tried calling her on the way, but she didn't answer or respond to my text. I just hoped that she was okay.

I pulled up to the hospital 15 minutes later and rushed inside. I didn't know where the hell to go to find her, so I parked near the emergency room entrance. I made my way through the automatic double doors and headed for the waiting room. I found her pacing the room in a panic.

"Baby, are you alright?" I asked.

Her face and neck were cut up like someone had just taken jabs at her with a sharp object.

"Zach what are you doing here?" she asked as she rushed up to me. I wrapped her in my arms as her body trembled.

"Brandie called me and said you were at the hospital. What happened to you?" I asked.

"It's a long story."

"Well, lucky for you, I got time. What happened? Why is your face and neck cut up like that?"

Before she could answer, Wynter, Tripp and Brandie rushed in. They made their way over to where we stood, worry written all over their faces. "Have you heard anything about O'Shea?" Tripp asked.

O'Shea? What the hell did Noelle's ex have to do with her being here?

"Did your ex do this to you? Did he hurt you?" I asked.

I saw her cast a look at Brandie and knew they were hiding something. A doctor walked out and asked for O'Shea's family. Everyone stepped up, but I stayed behind. I wasn't that nigga's family, so I didn't give a shit about what happened to him.

"I'm his best friend," Tripp said. "How is he?"

"Well, he was shot once in the left shoulder and grazed along his left temple. He's lost a lot of blood, but we were able to remove the bullet from his shoulder and he is stabilized. With a few months of therapy, he should make a full recovery," the doctor said.

"That's good news. Can we see him?" Tripp asked.

"Well, he's in recovery right now, but he'll be moved to a room in a couple of hours."

"Thank you doc."

The doctor made his way back through the double doors as everyone breathed a sigh of relief. When they turned to face me, I could see the worried look on Noelle's face. She walked over to me and immediately tried to explain.

"Were you with him?" I asked.

"It's not what you think babe," she said.

"Not what I think? How do you know what I'm thinking?" I asked. "Were you with him when he was shot? Is that why you have all those cuts on your face and neck?"

"Babe, can we talk about this in private?"

"No, we gon' talk about it right here, right now. Were you with him? Just answer me Noelle. I'm a grown man and I can handle the truth. Just be honest," I said.

"Yes, but we weren't together in the way that you're thinking."

"How do you know what I'm thinking? Stop trying to get in my head and think for me. What were you doing with him?" I asked.

I wasn't gonna lie, my heart was fucking breaking right now. I loved this girl, so to hear that she was with her ex and that she could've been killed when he got shot...

"He had asked to meet with me, so I wanted to find out what he wanted," she said.

"And what did he want?"

"I... I... I don't know. Before I could find out, someone started shooting at us. I got these cuts because the glass was flying everywhere, but I'm fine."

"We're just glad you're okay girl." Wynter said as she stepped in and hugged Noelle.

Brandie and Tripp hugged her too, but I didn't. I couldn't believe after everything that nigga had put her through, she was still running behind his ass. He had literally tried to break her spirit and everything, yet she still ran when he called. What was it about him?

"Well, I'm gonna be going. Y'all take care," I said as I made my way to the exit.

"Baby!" Noelle called behind me as I continued to walk away. "Babe! Please stop!"

I walked out the door as she continued to run behind me. It wasn't until I was outside that I turned around to face her. "What Noelle? What could you possibly have to say that you think I'd wanna hear right now?"

"I'm sorry. I love you, so please don't walk out on me," she said with tears in her eyes.

It pained me to see her that way, but I was hurt. "Noelle you still have unfinished business with that nigga after everything he put you through. I'm not going to play second fiddle to that nigga. I won't do it. If he's who you want to be with, then go be with him. I'll be fine."

"I don't want to be with him though. I want to be with you. You're the one I love Zach. I'm sorry I met with him, but if I learned anything from what happened today, it was that life is too short. You're the one I want to be with and I'm sorry," she said as she hugged me. "I'm so sorry."

I held her close even though my mind was telling me don't fall for it. I just knew that she wasn't through with that nigga, but I loved her.

"If you love me the way you say you do, let's go."

"You mean leave the hospital?"

"Yea. I don't wanna be here. I came here for you, not that nigga and you're fine, so I'm ready to go. Are you coming with me or not?" I asked.

"Yes, I'm coming with you. Just give me a minute to tell my friends I'm leaving," she said as she kissed me.

"I'll wait for you right here."

As she rushed back inside the hospital, I stood outside waiting for her. I wasn't about to let that nigga come between her and I, but I wasn't going to let him take my woman from me either. She and I would find a way to work this shit out. We had been spending way too much time together falling in love and shit, for us to let him win.

"Fuck that nigga!" I said.

Noelle came rushing out a couple of minutes later. She kissed me and put her hand in mine as we walked toward my car. I was confident that we could get past this as long as she stayed away from O'Shea.

Time would tell though. One thing I know for sure was if my woman was still fucking with that nigga, we were done!

Chapter one

Noelle

I was in the hospital waiting room pacing back and forth when Zach walked in. What was he doing here? I didn't call him. I looked over and Brandie had that look on her face that let me know she was the one who called him. Why would she do that? This wasn't his concern at all. I couldn't believe she betrayed me like that. The last thing I wanted was for him to be here right now when I wasn't sure what O'Shea's condition was. I just needed to know that he was going to be okay, but Zach wasn't having no parts of it. He was ready to go, so of course, I was going to go with him. He and I had been dating for a while now and he was my man. As much as I cared about O'Shea, he wasn't my concern anymore.

Since school had let out, Zach and I had been spending all of our free time together. Sometimes he had to help out at the family restaurant, so I'd hang out there until he was done. We hadn't had sex yet, but I knew one day it would happen. Tonight was probably not going to be that night. Zach was pretty upset with me for being with O'Shea.

"Do you realize that you could've been killed?" he asked as he started the car.

"Uh yea. Don't forget I was in the car when bullets started flying."

"Now is not the time for sarcasm babe. I'm serious."

"I'm serious too."

"What were you even doing with him anyway?" The dreaded question I was hoping that he wouldn't ask.

"I don't know."

"You don't know? What do you mean you don't know?" I asked. "You were in the car with him. How did you get there? Were you drugged? Did he drug you?"

"No, that's not what I'm saying.

"Then what the hell are you saying because none of this shit is making any sense to me. I thought the two of you were done..."

"We are done!"

"Then what were you doing with him?"

I didn't know how to answer that. The truth of the matter was that I shouldn't have been with O'Shea. He had dogged me out and used me for the past year. When I met Zach, it was like my whole world changed. I had no excuse for being with O'Shea... none at all.

"Answer me Noelle. Do you still have feelings for him? Were you still seeing him behind my back?"

"No, absolutely not! I have no excuse for being with him. He called and told me he needed help and I went. I knew it was wrong and that I should've said no, but I couldn't help it..."

"Because you still love him..."

"NO! That's not it at all. I don't know why I went to help him," I said. I really didn't know why I had come to O'Shea's aid... I just did.

"Noelle look, I care a lot about you, but if you're still hung up on that dude..."

"I'M NOT... I SWEAR!!"

"Well, you sure act like it. That nigga calls and you go running! What for? After everything that man put you through, why would you even answer the phone?"

No matter what I said, nothing would make sense to him. He felt that I should hate O'Shea after everything he did to me. But the truth was, I didn't. While I cared a lot about Zach, I was in love with O'Shea. I wasn't in love with him anymore, but I still cared a lot about him. He was my first love.

"Can I just apologize, and we agree to drop the subject? I know that I was wrong. I'm not disputing that. But can you look at the bigger picture? I could've been killed today." I said as the realization hit me like a ton of bricks. Tears slid down my eyes because I almost lost my life, and we were sitting here arguing about O'Shea instead of embracing the fact that I was alive.

"You're right. I'm sorry too," he said as he reached for my hand. "That must have been pretty scary for you."

"It was," I admitted as I nodded my head. "I had never been through anything like that before... EVER!! When those bullets started flying..." I couldn't even finish my statement because I was overcome with emotions.

As Zach pulled into his driveway, he hurried to park the car. He opened his arms and held me close as he rubbed my arm. "It's okay babe. You're okay."

"I know, but it was just so scary."

"All the more reason why you need to leave that nigga alone if he pulls through. You don't need that kind of stress or danger in your life. Do you know how hurt I would've been if things had turned out differently? I love you Noelle," he said as he lifted my chin with his finger.

"What?" I asked in disbelief. No man had ever told me they loved me before. Maybe my mind was playing tricks on me and I didn't hear what I thought I heard. I had been through something really traumatic.

"I said I love you. If something had happened to you, I would've been devastated."

He loved me. He really loved me! He slipped his tongue in my mouth and all I wanted to do was open my thick legs and give myself to him. I pulled out of his arms as he stared in confusion. "Can we go inside?" I asked, my voice barely above a whisper.

"Of course," he said as he grabbed his keys and stepped out of the car. I followed suit and he grabbed my hand and led me inside the house.

Once inside, I turned to him and asked, "Would you mind if I took a shower?"

"Not at all. Let me see if I can find a shirt for you," he said.

"You know darn well you don't have a shirt to fit me!"

"You may be surprised. You go hop in the shower and I'll find something for you to put on," he said.

I headed to the bathroom and turned on the shower. I stood in front of the mirror and looked at my reflection for a minute. I had been through hell today. I gasped when I saw the blood spot on my shirt. I hadn't noticed it that whole time, but I guess my mind was elsewhere. It wasn't my blood, so it had to be O'Shea's. I removed the shirt and tossed it in the trash. I didn't want that shirt anymore.

I removed the rest of my clothes and placed them on the counter. I would ask Zach to put them in the washer for me so I could have something to wear when I left here tomorrow. I stepped in the shower and allowed the warm water to cascade over me. It felt so good and relaxing. I needed this after the day that I had.

I reached for the bar of soap and brought it to my nose. I sniffed to make sure it wasn't a man's soap, and it wasn't. It smelled like Dove soap, so I began to rub it against my body. After about 15 minutes, I rinsed myself and all the grime from today's adventure down the drain. I turned the water off and stepped out of the tub. I reached for the plush towel and dried myself off. I was surprised that I could actually wrap the towel around myself. Damn, that was a big towel.

I walked out of the bathroom to find Zach sitting on the edge of the bed with a shirt in his hand. "I found something, but I didn't want to interrupt your time in the shower."

"Thank you," I said.

He stood up and looked at me with soft eyes. "You are so beautiful."

He reached for me and I went into his arms. Zach began kissing me with so much passion, it curled my toes. I had never been kissed like this before, not even by him on a previous occasion. As our tongues wrestled with each other, I found myself wanting more from him. He and I hadn't had sex before, but I wanted us to do it now. I wanted him to make love to me tonight. After everything I had been through today, I deserved to feel him inside me. I just hoped he was feeling the same way.

I dropped my towel on the floor. He took a step back and stared at my voluptuous body. At one time, I would've been insecure about my body, but those days were over. I had lost weight and Zach said he loved me. He often told me that he loved my fluffiness. As he stared at me, I smiled and placed my hands on my hips with my head held high.

"Damn! You are so fucking beautiful," he said with a smile as he stuffed his tongue in my mouth again. As the kiss deepened, he pushed me slowly on the bed. I laid back as he undressed quickly.

He then laid beside me and began kissing me while his hands roamed my body. He used his fingers to lightly pinch my nipples, turning me on even more. The only man I had ever been with was O'Shea, so I wondered if I'd be able to satisfy Zach. I mean, I wasn't that experienced.

When his lips left mine, I watched as they traveled down my fluffy belly. Even though I had lost some weight, I was still a bit chunky. Zach said he loved it, but I planned to lose more because it would make me a healthier person. When he reached my treasure, I just knew he wasn't about to do what I thought he was going to do. But he did.

He parted the lips of my pussy and began flicking his tongue over my love bud. Oh my God! I couldn't even describe the sensations that were coursing through my body. As he slid his tongue inside me, I gripped the sheets on the bed.

"Oh my God!" I cried out as my body shook.

He continued to suck and lick my vagina until my body calmed down. By the time he joined me in the bed, his dick was fully erect. I watched him reach over into the nightstand for a condom. He unwrapped it and rolled it on his meaty stick. I was pleasantly surprised by the shape of his dick because it wasn't too big or too small for me. It was actually just the right size for me.

He then got on top of me and inserted his dick inside me. That caused me to gasp for a second, but then my kitty adjusted and gripped his pole like a cat on a tree. As he rotated his hips slowly into me, I purred happily. He opened my legs wider and picked up the pace of his stroke. He had long strokes too because they were hitting that spot which sent shivers down my spine. I could barely keep it together as he went in. I felt amazing as he drove his hard shaft deeper inside me.

"Turn over babe," he whispered.

I did as he asked and repositioned myself on my hands and knees. As he got behind me, he smacked my butt. I giggled as he drove his dick inside me once again.

As he went harder and deeper, I found myself hollering like a she wolf. I had never been in a position like this before where I was really feeling him, and he was feeling me. He plunged deeper as he spread my butt cheeks apart. It felt like he had opened my pussy wider too. As I squealed louder, he continued to pleasure me.

Soon, both our bodies began to shake as we reached orgasmic pleasure that was out of this world. He removed the condom, wrapped it in a Kleenex tissue and dropped it in the trash can beside his bed. He reached in the drawer and pulled out a wet wipe for his hands and dick. Then he tossed it in the trash and reached over for me. I gladly went into his arms because after that good lovemaking we just had, I wanted to be held by him.

"Zach."

"Huh?"

"I love you too," I admitted.

He turned to look at me and asked, "Are you sure? I don't want you to feel like you have to say it because I said it."

"I'm sure. I've been knowing. I just was afraid of getting hurt."

"I'm never gonna hurt you babe... at least not on purpose."

"And I believe that."

"Please do. All I wanna do is love you, and now that I know you love me too..." He didn't finish his statement. Instead, he grabbed my face and kissed me hard on the lips.

Afterward, we fell asleep wrapped in each other's arms. I had never in my life been this happy. Now, my girls and I were all in love... I had Zach, Brandie had Nelson, and Wynter had Tripp. Things were looking up for the three of us.

Chapter two

O'Shea

Three days later...

I couldn't believe that nigga had shot me. What the fuck was he thinking? And then he did it in broad daylight. I had woken up from the hospital the next day and was discharged later that afternoon. I had been trying to reach Noelle ever since I was released, but she wasn't responding. I needed her to come through for me with this money because those niggas weren't playing. They really wanted me dead.

King wasn't the type of nigga that would understand if I said I didn't have it. I had already been spitting that line to him for a while now. I really didn't have the money and the only one I knew that could help me out with it was Noelle. But how the hell was I gonna get it if she wasn't answering.

I had tried reaching Tamika too, but she wasn't answering. As a matter of fact, she hadn't answered my calls for about three weeks. I didn't know what the hell was going on with these women, but something had to give. My arm was still in a sling from being nearly shot off. My doctor said that I'd have to go through physical therapy once the bandages came off in about six to eight weeks. Eight weeks with my arm in this shit. How the fuck was I supposed to work like that? How the hell was I gonna get the money to pay King's ass?

I decided to pay Tamika a visit. I wasn't finna drive all the way out there to see Noelle and she probably wouldn't be there. Tamika's place was closer than Noelle's, so I decided to go to her place. I could probably talk her into giving me the money since she was still sweet on me.

I knocked on Tamika's door and waited for her to open it. I almost shitted on myself when the door opened and it wasn't Tamika who answered. Instead, it was my boy Travis. What the fuck was Travis doing over here and why the fuck was he answering Tamika's door like this was his house? I mean, was this where his ass had been all this time? Somebody had some fuckin' explaining to do.

"Wassup O'Shea," he greeted.

"Whaddup nigga? Where Tamika at?" I asked.

"She's in the room getting dressed. She should be out in a minute."

In the room getting dressed? Where the fuck was she going?

"What da fuck you doing here Travis?" I finally asked the question I was dying to know the answer to.

"Tamika didn't tell you?"

"Tell me what?"

"I live here now," he answered with a smile.

"What the fuck you mean you live here now?"

"Just what I said. I know you noticed I ain't been at the crib lately. Oh, well maybe you haven't noticed. You probably ain't been at the crib because you still fucking all those ho's and having orgies and shit!" Travis said.

Oh shit! Now he had pissed me off. That nigga had a lot of fucking nerve talking about me having orgies when he was participating in them. Yea, I may have been a bit of a freak and shit, but that didn't mean I didn't care about her. Tamika was my boo... she knew that. We went way back and shit. How she gon' swap me out for some Trader Joe looking employee?

"Tamika! TAMIKA!" I yelled as I headed for the bedroom. I didn't even make it down the hall when Travis blocked my path.

"Aye dawg, I'ma need you to slow ya role. I told you she was gon' be out in a minute."

"Fuck you bruh! Why the fuck are you even here? Just get the fuck out so I can talk to my girl!" By this time, I was livid!

"Your girl?"

"That's what the fuck I said! You need me to spell it out for you?" I asked.

"Spell it out if you want to. Either way, I said SHE WILL BE OUT IN A FUCKIN' MINUTE!!" he shouted.

"What are you... her fuckin' bodyguard?" I asked. Before that nigga could answer, Tamika walked in.

She looked from me to Travis and rolled her fucking eyes. "Bae, what's going on?" she asked as she took a stand next to Travis. I watched him slip his arm around her waist and wanted to puke.

"O'Shea dropped by to see you. As usual, he acting like an ass and shit!" Travis responded.

"What are you doing here O'Shea? Why would you show up at my door without calling first?" she asked. She seemed angry, which made me angrier. What the fuck was she mad about?

"You got that nigga standing over there with his arm around you and you asking me what I'm doing over here? Why don't you tell me what the fuck is that nigga doing over here? I've been trying to reach yo ass for the past few weeks! I even called you when I got shot, but since you weren't picking up, I came by to see what was up. I had no idea y'all was creeping and shit behind my fuckin' back!!!"

"First of all, I'ma need you to watch how you fuckin' talk to my wife!" Travis said.

"Your wife? What the hell you talking about nigga?"

Did that nigga really just say that he married my ho'? This bitch was my ho'! I introduced his triflin' ass to her. What the fuck ever happened to the bro code?

"I told you that this is my wife. So, don't ever just drop by our house again without calling me first. And let me make myself perfectly clear about this shit here... whatever you and Tamika had going on before we got married is a done deal!"

Where the fuck was all this hostility coming from? If anybody should be pissed, it should've been me. What the hell was he so mad about?

I rubbed my goatee as I stared at the two of them looking like Tweedle Dee and Dumber. "So, let me get this straight. You married Tamika, a ho' we pulled a train on? You really trying to turn this ho' into a house..."

POW!

"I told you to watch what you say about my wife!" Travis said through clenched teeth.

I couldn't believe that he had married her. "You're really married?" I asked as I picked myself up off the floor.

The two of them stuck their ring fingers out, flashing their wedding rings. I swear I heard my mouth literally hit the floor.

"We got married two weeks ago and we're pregnant too!" Tamika informed me with a huge smile on her face.

"You're pregnant?"

"That's what I said."

"So, how do you know the kid is his? How do you know that ain't my kid?" I asked.

Tamika burst into laughter and responded, "Oh God! Hell no, this ain't your kid! I would never dream of having unprotected sex with you let alone have a baby by you! You're a dog O'Shea. You fuck everything in a skirt, and you've been doing it since forever. And FYI, Travis and I have been together since that first night," she said, smiling proudly like she wasn't a ho' that night.

"So, let me get this straight. You and Travis been fuckin' since I introduced y'all. Is that what the fuck y'all want me to believe?" I asked.

"You can believe it because it's the truth. To be honest, Travis and I were already familiar with each other before that night. We had actually met online a few months prior to your little introduction. I've been into him since we met but was afraid to trust him, especially after being around a dog like you. I'm glad you had him come over with you because it allowed us to spend some quality time together getting to know each other better," she explained.

"Well O'Shea, we would like to continue this little trip down memory lane with you, but we have a date tonight. With that being said, take care yourself and try not to get killed out there," Travis said as he opened the door.

That nigga had nerve to be funny! Wasn't shit funny about a nigga getting shot! I could've been killed and he out here making jokes. This nigga was supposed to be my brother, but this how he do me for some bitch who let us run a train on her. Yea, he was real fucked up for that shit.

Tamika stood in the middle of the living room with her hands on her hips smiling like she had just won the fucking lottery. I wanted to grab her by her damn neck and choke the life out of that nasty bitch. What kept me from doing that was Travis. That nigga punched me before even though I had my shoulder in a sling. My shit was already throbbing.

I just turned around and headed for the door. "Man, that's fucked up. We were supposed to be brothers. What happened to the bro code?"

"We're still brothers, so you shouldn't take this personal. We didn't do any of this to hurt you. We just fell in love. I just want you to be happy for us. I'd be happy for you," Travis responded.

"Fuck you ma nigga!" I said and walked out. He and Tamika could kiss my black ass.

Now, who was gonna give me the money to pay King's ass? I pulled out my phone and hit up the only other nigga I called my brother.

"Waddup?" answered Tripp.

"Aye Tripp, what you got going on?"

"Planning something special for Wynter. Waddup?"

"I need your help bro," I said, hoping he could hear the desperation in my voice.

He took a deep breath in and exhaled. I almost didn't wanna ask, but what choice did I have? Those niggas was out to kill me.

"What now?"

"I need 50 G's."

"Nigga what?"

"I owe King 50 G's or he's gonna kill me," I said.

"So, that's who shot you... King's crew?"

"Yea, and next time, I won't be lucky enough to talk about it."

"Nigga when are you gonna grow the fuck up and stop counting on other people to take care of your ass? I'm already letting you live in my spot rent free!"

"I know, and I appreciate it."

"I can't tell because you still out here doing dumb shit!"

"I'm sorry Tripp. Not everybody can be as successful as you," I said.

Tripp was my last hope, so the last thing I needed was for him to be looking down on me. He was either gonna help me or not, but I didn't need to hear about how big of a failure I was.

"You can be if you applied yourself."

"Look bro, I appreciate the advice, but what I really need is 50 grand. Now, can you help me out or not?" I asked. I wasn't trying to get smart with him like that, but I needed that money, or my ass was dead.

"I'll help you out, but I swear, this is the last time. You need to grow the fuck up and handle your damn business," he said.

"Thank you bro. I knew I could count on you."

"Yea, this time. Don't count on it next time. I'ma send the shit to your PayPal."

"Make sure you send enough so that I have 50 G's after they take their cut," I said.

"Damn nigga! Are you broke broke?" he asked.

"Duh! Why you think I'm calling you?"

"Damn! Aight!" He didn't bother saying goodbye. He just hung the phone up on me.

About 20 minutes later, I got an alert from PayPal saying I had money. I checked my account and the money had been deposited... $52,000. I called Jasper and let him know I had the damn money, so they could get off my fucking back. By that evening, all the money had been paid and I lived to see another day. I just had to make better choices because my life depended on it.

Chapter three

Tripp

When my phone started ringing and O'Shea's name popped up, I knew I should've ignored it. I shouldn't have answered because I knew he was gonna fuck up the good vibes I had going on. I was just tired of bailing his ass out of debt. I knew darn well he wasn't gonna ask his dad for help with his drug debt. He needed to get it together because I wasn't going to keep helping him out. When I stated that was the last time, I meant that shit.

I had something special planned for Wynter tonight. I sent her to the spa so she could get the total package, complete with manicure, pedicure, facial, massage, hairstyle and makeup. I had something really special planned for us and I wanted everything to be perfect. I hired people to set up a huge tent on the beach. Soft music played from speakers of the CD player and there strands of lights everywhere to add to the romantic ambience I was trying to set for my lady.

I hired a chef to prepare a special dinner for us. As I waited for Wynter to join me under the tent, my nerves had me pacing nervously back and forth. When the tent finally opened and she walked in, I could see why she had kept me waiting. She literally took my breath away.

She wore a dress the color of orange sherbet with the topaz and diamond necklace and earrings set I had given to her. Her hair was swept to the side with loose tendrils that framed her beautiful face. She was absolutely stunning!! As she walked toward me, my heartbeat sped up.

"You look beautiful!" I said as I kissed her.

"Thank you. This is so beautiful babe! I can't believe you did all this for me!" she said in awe.

"As beautiful as this might be, it pales in comparison to you," I said.

I pulled out her seat and she sat down. I took my seat across from her. The waiter placed our meals on the table, lifted the lids and popped open the bottle of champagne. He poured each of us a glass and stood near the entrance of the tent.

"To us," I said as we clinked our glasses together. We each took a sip and began eating our food. The chef had prepared blackened catfish, coconut shrimp, garlic and herb mashed potatoes and for dessert, Southern peach cobbler a la mode.

"You really outdid yourself," she said.

"I wanted tonight to be special."

"You succeeded. No one has ever done anything like this for me before."

"I'm not just anyone," I said.

"You got that right."

We continued to chat as we ate our food. Then I decided it was time to break out with the real reason why we were here. Before I could lose my nerve, I stood up from my seat and took the couple of steps to get the where Wynter was seated. I got down on one knee and took her left hand in mine.

"What's going on?" she asked, surprise evident on her beautiful face.

"I've waited my whole life for a woman as beautiful and loving as you. I knew from the moment I laid eyes on you that I had to have you. Even though you gave me a hard time at first, eventually you gave me a chance to prove to you what kind of man I am. I want to have kids and grow old with you. I want to travel the world with you and explore with you. But I want to do those things with you as my wife," I said.

"Oh my God Tripp! Are you serious right now?"

"As a heart attack," I smiled as I reached in my pants pocket. I pulled out the burgundy velvet ring box and opened it. The iridescent blue light shined on the sparkling emerald cut pink diamond ring. The ring was six carats with diamond baguettes on each side and set in platinum. I knew it was extravagant, but I wanted something exquisite enough to match her beauty.

I held the ring over her left ring finger and asked, "Wynter Nicole Caswell, will you marry me?"

"Yes! Yes! A million times yes!" She was so excited as I slipped the ring on her finger. I literally lifted her off her feet and kissed her with all the love I had inside me.

"So, I need to ask you something."

"Something else?"

"I was wondering if you would consider moving in with me now. I mean, if you'd rather wait until after the wedding, that's fine too," I said, not wanting to rush her. "It's just that I have a huge house and I can't wait to fill it with you and our kids. No pressure though, so if you choose to stay at your place until after we're married I'm okay with that. Just know that I love you so much and I can't wait to start my life with you."

She wrapped her arms around my waist, looked up into my eyes and said, "Do you know how much I love you? Do you know how happy you have made me? I want to spend the rest of our lives making you happy, so of course I'll move in with you. I can pack my things and be there by the end of next week. How about that?"

"That would be awesome! I don't think I've ever been this happy in my whole life." I lifted her up again and she wrapped her legs around my waist as we sealed our engagement with a kiss. "Give me one minute." I dropped her down to her feet and walked over to the guy I hired to be my waiter for the evening. I gave him two crisp one hundred- dollar bills. "There's another three of those if you arrive at eight tomorrow to clean up before the people come to remove the tent."

"Yes sir, I'll be here," he said and scurried out.

I walked back over to where Wynter was standing and picked her up, kissing her to the spot where I had them lay out a makeshift bed. I dropped her slowly onto the pillows and climbed on top of her. I kissed her hungrily as I felt up her dress. When my fingers found what they were looking for, I inserted two into her warm center. She was already wet which made my dick harden immediately. I plunged my fingers in and out of her as she moaned against my lips.

I couldn't wait to get inside her, so I quickly removed my clothes as she did hers. I got back down and climbed on top of her, allowing my shaft to find its way inside a place it called home. As I pressed forward, she hissed as I held her hips upward.

"It feels so good," she moaned.

I continued to plunge inside her until her body shook. I felt her cream seep out onto my dick. As it traveled down my dick, I sped up the process to get mine. She moaned louder as I put her feet on my shoulders. I drove my dick into her G-spot with fervor as she wound her hips against me. Finally, my orgasm rushed out in an array of bullets as I sprayed her insides.

I collapsed beside her and held her close while we breathed like we just finished competing in a marathon. After a few minutes, she asked, "So, you wanna go up to the house? I really need a shower after all that sweating we just did."

"Yea, I could use a shower."

We proceeded to put our clothes back on. "You sure it's okay that this tent is set up out here for the night?" she asked.

"It's fine. I got a permit for it and everything. They'll be by in the morning to clean up and remove it," I explained.

"What a man I have in you. You make dreams come true," she said as she entered my arms again. I planted a kiss on her lips and hugged her tight.

"This is only the beginning babe... only the beginning."

We held hands as we walked back to the house. I noticed Brandie's car in the driveway. We walked in, but no one was in the living room to greet us. As we made our trek down the hallway to the master bathroom, we could hear soft moans coming from Brandie's room.

Craving the Love of a F**k Boy 2

Wynter pressed her fingers to her lips as we continued tiptoeing to her room.

The shower led to more sex and then we fell asleep wrapped in a circle of love.

Chapter four

O'Shea
Two months later...

Having that nigga off my back was the best feeling in the world. Not only that, but I had gotten that sling off my arm and my shoulder was much better. I had been receiving physical therapy for the past three weeks and the doctor was confident that my shoulder would be back to normal in a few more weeks. I was excited about that. I just wish my personal life was going better, but in time things would shape up. At least that was my hope. Noelle had been running with that lil nigga ever since I got out of the hospital. I had hoped that the shit would've run its course by now, but nope...she was still stuck on stupid for that nigga. I couldn't believe how sexy she had become since losing that weight. She lost about a hundred pounds and now, she was out there giving my pussy to some other nigga.

Tamika and Travis had disrespected me in the worst way by getting married. What the hell was happening to my life right now? Nothing was going right, and I couldn't figure out why. All I knew was that something had to give.

I called Sassy and asked if she could meet me at my place.

"Uh, I don't think so..." she declined.

"Well, either you come here, or I'll go there. Either way, we are going to see each other tonight," I demanded.

She already knew not to play with me. "I don't want to see you O'Shea. Last time we were together, you almost killed me!"

"That was an accident," I said.

Okay, I could admit that I had gotten a little too rough with her. But shit, I had apologized and everything. Why the hell was she still holding on to that shit? It was like she couldn't accept the fact that I was sorry and let the shit go.

"Your behavior hasn't been the same..."

"Look, how many times I gotta say sorry? Are you coming or not? Because if not, I'm gonna get in my car and be on my way."

"I'm coming," she finally said.

"Good. Don't be too long."

Half an hour later, I saw her car pull in. I had been watching for her, so as soon as she got out of the car, I opened the door to let her in.

"What took you so long?" I barked.

"I came right over O'Shea, so I don't know what you're talking about," she said as she rolled her eyes upward.

I wasted no time ripping her clothes off once I had her inside. I dropped my robe and pulled her toward the bedroom. She always said how she liked it rough, so rough was what she'd get. I shoved her on the bed, dropped to my knees and began to suck her pussy.

She moaned as I ran my tongue up and down her slit. She began to grind her hips, fucking my mouth in the process. I nibbled on her clit causing her to wince in pain. She knew I didn't like when she did that shit. She had her pussy all up in my nose and shit.

"Ow!" she screamed and jumped up. "Are you crazy? Why the fuck would you do that?"

I didn't bother to answer. I simply smiled and stared at her like she was the crazy one. She tried to get off the bed and make a run for it, but I grabbed her and threw her back down on the bed.

"Where you going huh? I thought you liked it rough?" I said.

"O'Shea, please let me go... you're hurting me!" she cried.

I shoved my big dick into her pussy and fucked her with all my might as she pleaded for me to stop. I gripped her neck and choked her while I was fucking her. She begged me to stop, but I continued until her face turned purple. I removed my hand from her throat, but continued to push in and out of her roughly.

As she begged me to stop, I pulled out and flipped her over onto her stomach. I wanted to fuck her doggie style, but the bitch refused to get on all fours. Well, what I was about to do next was her own damn fault. I spread her ass cheeks and spit on her asshole. I shoved my thumb inside her ass as she cried out.

"O'Shea no! Please don't do this! I already told you that I don't do anal!" she cried.

"Oh, so now you wanna play nice?" I teased.

She got on her hands and knees and arched her back. "I'm sorry. Just please, don't do it!"

Shit, she had me fucked up. I spit on her asshole again before shoving my dick inside her asshole. She screamed as I watched the head disappear in her.

"Ow, O'Shea! Please stop!" she screamed.

She tried to push me out of her, but I wouldn't budge. She should've done what she was supposed to do. "You got a tight asshole," I teased.

She had tears running from her eyes as she cried in pain. I removed my dick from her ass and slammed it inside her pussy. I wrapped my arm around the side of her and played with her clit. Finally, I released my sperm all over her fat ass. I smacked her on the other cheek with my hand.

She tried to push me away from her, but I grabbed her by the hair. I pulled her body against mine, causing the semen to smash between our sweaty bodies. I kissed her neck softly as she cried and moaned at the same time. I sunk my teeth into her skin as she cried out. I bit and sucked until I tasted her blood in my mouth.

"Ow O'Shea, please stop! I'll do anything you want just stop!" she begged.

I turned her around, so she was facing me. I pinned her arms behind her back and kissed her hard, forcing my tongue into her mouth. As our tongues danced in each other's mouths, I played with her pussy. She moaned softly as my kisses trailed to her neck. Once again, I bit down hard on her neck. She winced and tried to push away from me. When I removed my mouth from her flesh, I felt blood dripping from my mouth.

I wiped my lips with the back of my hand. "I want you to suck my dick," I said as I licked her lips. Tears ran down her cheeks as I pressed my lips to hers. "If you even think about biting my shit, I will snap your fuckin' neck. UNDERSTAND?!"

She nodded and began to stroke my dick in her soft hands. She then took my dick in her mouth and sucked it until it became hard again. When she started gagging on my dick, I gripped her hair and pushed her back on the bed. I lifted one of her legs and inserted my dick into her sore pussy. I gripped her hips and fucked her as hard as I could.

I knew what I was doing was wrong, but I didn't care. I was sick and tired of people treating me like shit and somebody had to pay for it. I continued this rough sex with Sassy until well into the night. When I had finally worn myself out, I collapsed on the bed and fell asleep. I was exhausted like a muthafucka. Who knew fucking could be so tiring?

I didn't know how long I had been sleeping, but I woke up because some motherfucker was banging on my fucking door like the gotdamn police.

BANG! BANG! BANG!

I jumped out of bed, wondering where the hell Sassy was. She wasn't in the bed, so why the hell she didn't answer the damn door?

"SASSY!" I called as I threw on a shirt and some sweatpants. "SASSY!"

The banging persisted, so I went to answer the door. Imagine how my heart dropped when I pulled the door open and there was a police officer and two detectives on my doorstep. What the fuck did they want? I knew I hadn't done shit wrong, so I was confused as to why they were here.

"I'm Detective Clark and this is my partner, Detective Parker. Are you O'Shea Washington?" he asked.

"Yes. What can I do for you detective?" I asked.

"We'd like to come in and ask you a few questions if that's okay," Detective Parker said.

I didn't know what the fuck they were here for, but I had nothing to hide. I stepped aside and allowed them to enter my home. I just hoped I wouldn't regret the decision.

Detective Parker spoke first. "We received a call an hour ago pertaining to a young woman who claimed to have been sexually assaulted in this complex."

"What? Somebody was raped in our complex?" I asked.

"Yes. Perhaps you might know the victim. Her name is Rhianna Thomas."

"Who?" I asked. Who the fuck was Rhianna Thomas and what made them think I knew her? I ain't never heard of that name before in my life.

"Sir, are you going to tell us that you don't know Rhianna Thomas?" Detective Clark asked with an attitude.

"I honestly don't know who you're talking about!"

"So, you don't know a light skinned, blonde haired woman named Rhianna Thomas?" Detective Parker asked. I guess I was still sitting there with a blank expression on my face because he pulled out his phone. He turned the phone to me. "Do you know this woman?"

Damn. He was talking about Sassy! Shit, I didn't know Rhianna was her real name. We had never discussed her government name.

"Oh, you mean Sassy... yea, I know her. I just didn't know her government name was Rhianna. You said someone raped her?" I asked.

"Yes, she was raped last night."

Now, I was confused. Sassy was with me last night, so who the... wait a minute. I just knew that these niggas wasn't trying to say I raped her.

"That's impossible because she was with me last night," I said.

"Right. That fits right into the timeline since she told us that you did it," Detective Parker stated.

"Oh, hell naw!! That's bullshit!"

"So, you weren't with her at all last night?" Detective Clark asked.

"No, I was with her, but I didn't rape her. I mean, do I look like the type of nigga that would need to rape a woman to get some pussy?" I asked. I couldn't believe that Sassy had turned me in to the cops.

"So, you didn't rape her?"

"Hell naw! Look, she and I get together from time to time and engage in role playing. Sometimes, we get a little rough... sometimes, very rough. But I didn't rape her!" I said.

"So, what you're saying is that you guys were together last night, but you didn't sexually assault her?"

"That's exactly what I'm saying! I don't have to sexually assault anybody!" I argued.

"So, let me see if I understand this correctly. You were with Miss Thomas last night. You guys were role playing which led to rough sex. Is that right?" Detective Clark asked.

"Yes, that's exactly right! I met her a few months ago shaking her ass at the strip club. Did y'all know she was a stripper?"

"No, we weren't aware of that," Detective Parker said.

"Well, she is... a damn good one I might add. Anyway, she and I have been role playing ever since the first night we met," I said with a smile. "She's very good at her job."

The two detectives looked at each other, then back at me. "Well, regardless of where she works, Miss Thomas was assaulted last night and she's accusing you of being her attacker," Detective Parker said.

"I didn't do that shit!" I argued.

"Well, we're gonna need you to put your hands behind your back, Mr. Washington."

"For what?" I asked.

"You're under arrest for rape."

"The fuck? I just told you that I didn't do it!"

"Right, but you've been accused, and we have a warrant for your arrest. You will be able to tell the district attorney your side. It's gonna be up to the prosecutor's office and the grand jury to decide if they want to pursue the case. For right now, I need you to turn around and put your hands behind your back," Detective Parker said.

"What happened to her word against mine?" I asked.

"It's still her word against yours, Mr. Washington. Unfortunately, she has handprints around her neck, bite marks, bruises and a statement that accuses you of assaulting her. Now, you have the right to remain silent. Anything you say, can and will be used against you in a court of law. You have the right to an attorney. If you cannot afford an attorney, one will be appointed to you by the court. Do you understand these rights as I have read them to you?" the detective asked.

"Yes!" They slapped the cuffs on me and escorted me out of my place. That was some crazy shit. I knew I had gotten a little rough with her last night, but damn. For her to call the cops on me... that fucking snitch!

Chapter five

Sassy aka Rhianna

I couldn't believe that O'Shea had treated me that way. Why would he do me like that? I had never done anything that deserved him treating me that way. As soon as I heard him snoring, I slid out of the bed quietly. I almost pissed on myself when he stretched his arm out. I prayed that he wouldn't feel that I wasn't there. I quickly slipped my feet in my shoes and grabbed the robe he wore earlier when I arrived. I snuck quietly out the door and continued tiptoeing until I was out of view from his apartment.

I was beat up mentally and physically. My head was pounding from when he pulled it back. I had bruises and bite marks all over the upper and lower parts of my body. My butt hole felt like it was split open by an 18-wheeler. My neck was sore, and it felt swollen. I couldn't even talk normally. The sound of my voice came out hoarse.

I dragged myself across the parking lot slowly trying to get to my car. When I felt a hand touch on my shoulder, I screamed because I thought it was O'Shea.

"Are you alright?" an elderly woman asked.

"Yes, I'm fine," I said as I continued walking toward my car.

"I can call the police for you if you like honey. You don't look alright," the woman said.

I just collapsed on the ground and started crying. The little old lady put her arms around me and yelled for someone to call the police. A short time later, I was surrounded by residents of the complex and soon, I heard sirens approaching.

"It's going to be alright honey. The police and paramedics are here to help you," she said as she stroked my hair.

The police and ambulance arrived, and asked me questions which I couldn't answer. They finally shoved me into the back of the ambulance and drove me to the hospital. The only thing I did confirm for them was that I was attacked and raped.

At the hospital, I was examined by the doctor. A rape kit was done, and I was treated for my wounds. I was asked to pee in a cup and blood and STD tests were performed. Of course, the rape kit showed that I had bruising on my thighs and my rectum had been torn. Thank God my other tests proved negative for STDs. Dr. Goldstein allowed the detectives to come in and speak to me once the exam was done.

"Miss Thomas, can you tell us what happened to you?"

"I was raped! Didn't the doctor tell you that?" I asked.

"Yes, but we need to hear it from you," Detective Clark said.

"I was raped!"

"Do you know who your attacker is?"

"Yea," I said.

I wasn't sure if I should tell them that O'Shea was the one who attacked me. I didn't know how he would retaliate against me once the cops went to arrest him. But I had to report this. I didn't have a choice and O'Shea had gone way too far. I still didn't know why he would do this to me. I had never done anything to him for him to think this was okay. I was worried about his mind frame these days. I believe he needed help.

"His name is O'Shea Washington. He lives in the complex I was found at... apartment 2B," I said.

"Can you tell us exactly what happened between the two of you?"

"Do I have to do this now?"

"We'd prefer that you do. Most often, it's best to recount the events right after because sometimes victims tend to forget pertinent details the longer they wait," the detective said.

So, for the next half hour, I spoke to them about everything that O'Shea had put me through. Pictures were taken of the bite marks on my neck and shoulder, to the bruising on my thighs and the bite marks on my breasts. O'Shea had really done a number on me and I was glad I had run into that elderly lady. If it wasn't for her, he would've gotten away with what he had done.

Finally, I was released and sent home with instructions to care for my wounds, a shot for pain, and prescriptions for pain medication. I was also given a tetanus shot because of the bite marks O'Shea had inflicted on me. I was also given an HIV test due to O'Shea breaking my skin when he bit me. Those results would be available within the next week or so, but I wasn't worried. I knew that O'Shea didn't have HIV.

I contacted an Uber driver to take me back to O'Shea's place so I could get my car. I hope he was nowhere around because I never wanted to see him again. I had been in an abusive relationship before, so I wasn't trying to get in another one. I didn't love O'Shea, so there was no way I was going to allow him to use and abuse me that way. Abuse was the reason I ended things with Clifton. Just looking at the bruises on my body brought me back to a place I thought I'd never go again. As I sat in the back seat of the Uber driver's car, I thought about when I reached my breaking point with Clifton.

Three years ago...

Clifton and I had been in a relationship for about two years. Two years too long if you asked me. However, I was totally in love with him. I would've done anything for him, and I tried my best to please him. I cooked, cleaned, sucked his dick, and freaked him in bed. The problem we had was that he didn't like me dancing at the strip club. We argued about that on a regular basis, but if I was to be completely honest, I tried other jobs.

That's right. I quit working at the club twice to try working at different jobs just to save my relationship. But I was used to making a certain amount of money every week. Those jobs were paying five to six hundred every two weeks. He couldn't be seriously wanting me to work a job that paid that much in a week when I made that much in a night at the strip club. But he was serious. He hated my job as a dancer, but I felt that if he met me there and didn't have a problem with it, why would he have a problem with it a year later.

We argued back and forth for six months before he started putting his hands on me. He wanted me to see things his way and that was the only way. When he hit me the first time, he immediately apologized but said he did it because I wasn't listening to how he felt. I forgave him, but then it happened again. Once again, he apologized, and all was forgiven. But when he kept doing it, I eventually began throwing hands back. I wasn't a weak woman by any means, so if he was going to hit me, I was going to hit him back.

That last night was the worst he had ever beat me. I had come in around three that morning from the club. I was exhausted. All I wanted to do was climb in bed and sleep. I had already showered at the club, so I only had to dress for bed.

I changed into some booty shorts and a wife beater and climbed in bed next to Clifton. As soon as I tried to snuggle with him, he threw my hands off him. Rather than feed into the shit, I turned my back and moved closer to my side.

"Oh, that's how it is huh?" he asked.

"I'm tired Cliff. All I'm trying to do is get some sleep."

"You wouldn't be so damn tired if you wasn't at that fuckin' club til three in the morning shaking yo ass for other niggas!"

"Why do we have to talk about this now? I just told you that I was tired," I said.

"I don't give a fuck if you're tired! You wasn't too tired to twist that big ass for those niggas though! Now that you home, all of a sudden you so damn tired!"

I knew he was trying to argue with me, and I didn't want to hear that. We had been having the same fight for the past six months and I didn't wanna do it no more. I just wanted to relax and get some sleep. Why was he trying to argue with me at three in the morning?

"I've been tired Cliff and I'm tired of explaining why I still work at the club! If that's it, I'm going to bed!"

"I want you to quit that job!"

"I'm not gonna quit the job... PERIOD!!" I said. "Maybe I should sleep on the sofa tonight." I slipped out of bed and grabbed my pillow. I was gonna go to the living room to sleep since it was obvious I wasn't gonna get any here.

"Oh bitch! You think you gon' just walk away from me like that!" He hopped out of bed so fast I hadn't had time to blink.

He punched me in the back of the head and that sent me flying to the floor. How could I not hit the floor? Cliff was a big dude. That punch knocked me off my damn feet. As I began sprawling on the floor in an effort to get up, he climbed on top of me and started punching me in the face. He punched, beat and choked me until I passed out. Then he took me to the bathroom, placed me in the tub and turned the shower on.

When I came to, he was sitting in the corner of the bathroom crying his eyes out. I could barely see out of my right eye and my left one was closed completely. I coughed and he jumped up and ran over to me. As he approached, I lifted my hands to ward off any hits he might try to hit me with again.

Instead of hitting me, he lifted me up out of the tub, cleaned the blood off my face and brought me to bed. I was in awe to *what he had done because he had never hurt me this badly. He held on to me and apologized throughout the morning. I didn't say anything. As soon as he left me alone, I contacted the police. There was no way he was getting away with that. I was taken to the hospital and Clifton was taken to jail.*

As of today, he's still incarcerated for what he did to me. So, regardless of how O'Shea felt, he deserved to be locked up just like Clifton was. No woman should have to deal with that type of abuse from any man.

Chapter six

O'Shea

I couldn't believe I had gotten arrested because I gave Sassy what she wanted. Those niggas knew I didn't rape that bitch, yet here I was. As I sat in the interrogation room waiting for them to come see about me, I wondered once again, who I could call to get me out of this situation. I wanted to call Noelle, but she hadn't been responding to my calls. Tamika was in her own shit and Tripp had told me not to call him anymore. I thought about calling my dad, but I knew how disappointed he would be in me.

The detectives walked in one and said, "We are going to process and book you into county jail."

"I didn't do anything. I'm telling you that y'all have the wrong one!"

"We're just doing our jobs."

"Well, can I get my one phone call?"

"Yea, sure." They left and one of them returned with a rotary phone. I had no idea people still used these phones. He plugged it into the wall outlet and left the room again.

As I picked up the phone, I looked at it as I struggled to figure out who I was going to call. I finally decided to contact Noelle. Hopefully, she would come see about me. The phone rang until it went to voicemail twice. The third time I called, she finally picked up... at least, I thought it was her.

"Hello," came the male voice.

"Yo, can I speak to Noelle please?"

"Why do you keep calling my girl? She doesn't want anything to do with you after you almost got her killed!"

"Listen here homie. You don't know anything about what me and Noelle got going on," I said. The nerve of that nigga to be coming at me like he knew me. He didn't know shit about me.

"I know enough to know that you were using her. She's happy now. I'ma ask you again to not call her anymore. Matter of fact, I'ma have her block yo number once you hang up," he said.

"This ain't even my number muthafucka, so block that shit all you want! Ol' insecure ass nigga!" I hung the phone up after that.

I called the only other person who had always been there for me. I knew he said he wouldn't help me anymore, but we were brothers. Tripp wouldn't leave me in here, would he?

"Hello?" he answered, sounding unsure of who was calling him.

"Tripp, it's O'Shea."

"Nigga what you doing calling me from the police station?"

"Look, I got myself in a little pickle over here. I need you to come down here and bail me out," I said.

"Bail you out? You mean you got arrested?"

"Yea, but they ain't got nothing on me! I just need a good lawyer to come down here and talk her or his shit!"

"Remember what I told you when I bailed you out with that 50 grand?"

"Tripp, I need you bruh!"

"I know, but what you really need is to grow the hell up. Maybe some time behind bars will get yo mind right!"

"What?! You're kidding right?"

"Nah, I ain't kidding. I'm tired of this shit. You should be old enough to know right from wrong..."

"I do! That bitch that got me arrested is a ho'! She lied to the cops, so they picked me up! But I ain't do nothing!"

"It's always somebody else's fault but yours. You need to leave to take accountability for your actions. Grow the hell up man!"

"Tripp please bro, if you help me out of this shit, I promise..."

"I know... you promise to grow up. You promise not to call me anymore. You've made so many promises to me that your promises don't mean shit to me no more! Like I said, maybe some time behind bars will help you grow up and do right."

With that, I heard a click in my ear. "TRIPP! TRIPP!" I banged the phone on the hook. This nigga had always been there for me. How the hell was he gon' just leave me locked up in here?

The two detectives walked back in.

"Mr. Washington, we need to get you booked in."

"Man, I didn't do this shit. I swear!"

"So, if you didn't sexually assault the victim, why would she say you did?"

"Did she actually say that I sexually assaulted her? I mean, did she say those words, or did you guys hear what you wanted to hear?" I asked in a cocky manner because I knew that Sassy wouldn't have said that about me. She knew what time it was with us. She knew how we got down. Last night wasn't our first rodeo like that.

"She actually did say that. She also showed us the bruises, bite marks, and handprints around her neck, which she said you are responsible for," Detective Parker said.

"Nah, I know for a fact she didn't say that shit because I didn't do anything she didn't want me to do," I said.

"So, you're admitting that you did bite and choke Miss Thomas?"

"Yes, but she wanted me to. I told y'all she liked it rough!" I said.

"So, what you're telling me is that Miss Thomas wanted you to do this to her?" Detective Parker asked as he produced picture after picture after picture of Sassy. Damn, I hadn't hurt her that bad, had I?

Her neck had purple fingerprints intertwined around it. She had huge bite marks on her shoulder and neck. That shit looked so swollen and purple, like it was infected or something. That shit looked horrible. How the fuck was I responsible for that shit? We were having fun, but I didn't do that shit! That bitch was trying to set me up!

"Look, I didn't do that shit! None of that shit looks like anything I would've done!" I said.

"Well you did say she liked it rough. Maybe you don't know your own strength," Detective Clark said.

"I know I didn't do that shit! Look, I might be a freaky nigga behind closed doors, but I'm not abusive to women!" I said.

"Yea, we've heard that before."

"I'm serious though," I said.

KNOCK! KNOCK! KNOCK!

They opened the door and there stood an attractive female officer. She was fine as fuck. Shit, I hoped she wanted some because she could definitely get it.

"Captain wants to see you Byron," she said.

Detective Clark left the room and the female detective sat down. I wondered if this was some type of ploy to get me to implicate myself with a beautiful woman. Shit, they had the wrong one because I'd never throw my own ass under the bus that way.

"Mr. Washington, tell me this. As attractive as you are, why would you feel the need to sexually assault any woman?" the female asked.

"I'm sorry, but what'd you say your name was?"

"Officer Brinks."

"Well, Officer Brinks, as I was telling these other two detectives, I ain't never had to sexually assault any woman. I didn't do that to that woman. She and I had sex... hot, sweaty, rough sex. She begged me to fuck her as hard as I could with my 10-inch dick. She begged me to put it in her ass. She begged me to choke her. She asked me to bite her hard. She wanted that shit and I had no problem giving it to her!" I said as I stared into her eyes while licking my lips.

I could see her lip trembling as sweat started to appear on her forehead and upper lip. I watched her shift in her chair and I could almost hear her heart beating wildly behind her shirt.

"But did she ask you to leave those awful bruises and welts on her body?" Detective Parker asked.

"Hell yea, she wanted that shit! I wasn't trying to leave any marks like that on her, but I guess I loss control. I was just fucking her so hard, but she still kept yelling for me to fuck her harder. So, I thought if I bit her she would feel more of the pain she wanted to feel. Trust me she loved it and was into it. I've known this woman for months. You just met her. She loved every bit of what I did to her last night," I said as I stared into the female detective's eyes. "She loved every single minute of it! You are really making a mistake arresting me."

I could tell the female officer was feeling some kind of way. She knew I didn't rape that girl. Shit, I bet she wanted some of this dick her damn self.

"Mr. Washington, no one cares about the size of your penis," Detective Parker said. "We're investigating the sexual assault of Miss Thomas."

"I'm telling you Detective Parker, there was no sexual assault. That bitch gave me the pussy... point blank PERIOD! I don't know why you are having such a hard time understanding what I'm telling you. Y'all just wanna lock niggas up for no damn reason!"

"Why would she say you assaulted her if you didn't?" Detective Brinks inquired.

"Shit, I don't know! You'll have to ask her that shit!" I said.

"Take him and book him," the detective said to the female.

She stood up and even though I wasn't wild about being booked and processed, I went with her. As we walked down the hall, I said, "Now, you know damn well I didn't rape that woman."

"I know no such thing," she responded.

"C'mon, do I look like the type of nigga that would have to steal pussy?"

"Good looks deceive people all the time."

"Oh, so you think I'm good looking?" I asked with a smile. "You know that you can get it too, right?"

She didn't respond. She continued walking me to the processing area in silence.

"Just let me know when you're ready for me to widen your sugar walls with this big dick. Have you ever had a threesome? How about a foursome? I'm a real freak and can give it to you any way you want," I said.

"Mr. Washington, can you shut the hell up please?" she asked with an attitude.

"Damn, a nigga just trying to give you some satisfaction."

"For your information, I get satisfied every night by my husband."

"I bet his dick ain't big as mine though. I bet he don't lick your pussy all the way to your asshole. I bet he don't suck on your pearl until you..."

"MR. WASHINGTON!!" she yelled as she stopped walking. "Please evoke your right to remain silent."

I didn't say anything else, but I knew she wanted some.

I was in jail for three fucking days before I was bailed out. I didn't know who the fuck paid my bail and I didn't give a shit I was just glad to be out and free. Three days in that motherfucker was way too long for me. I knew when I left that Detective Brinks would be looking me up. She had to. I gave her plenty to think about while I was locked up.

I made sure she caught me a couple of times with my dick on hard. I saw the lust in her eyes. And no matter what she told me, I knew her husband wasn't hitting it right. The first place I went when I left the jail was Sassy's place. I needed her to tell me why the fuck she got me locked up. She knew she enjoyed that shit.

I knocked on her door, putting my finger over the peephole, so she couldn't see me on the other side. I hoped that even if she didn't know who was at the door, she'd still open it and she did. As soon as she cracked that door, I pushed it open. As soon as she saw me, she tried to take off running, but I was just too fast. I closed the door shut and pulled her to me.

"O'Shea, I didn't say anything! I swear!"

I didn't respond as I grabbed her throat and choked her while licking her face.

"The fuck you mean you didn't say anything? I wouldn't have spent the last three days in jail if you had kept your fuckin' mouth closed!" I taunted.

She tried to speak but couldn't because my hand was still wrapped around her neck. I finally released her neck and asked, "Why would you tell those pigs that I raped you?"

Tears streamed from her eyes as she stared at me, fearful of what I might do next. My dick began to get hard because of the control that I had over her. "I swear I didn't say anything about rape. I was going to my car that morning and this old woman approached me and asked if I was okay. I told her that I was, but when she noticed the bite marks and bruises, she called the police. Before I knew it, I was in the back of an ambulance on my way to the hospital. They did a rape kit and said that I was raped. I didn't tell them that!" she said.

"Okay, let's say I believe you. How did they get my name?" I asked, playing along with her. I didn't believe shit she was telling me.

"I don't know. That wasn't the first time I visited your apartment though. Maybe someone saw me coming out of it and they told the police."

"That doesn't make sense, but okay."

I was done arguing with her because my dick was super hard. I grabbed her by her hair and stuffed my tongue deep inside her mouth. I tore off the lace panties she had on under that short ass gown and stroked her pussy. She whimpered from my touch. I was sure that sex with me was the last thing she wanted, but she was gonna have to give up the pussy. I stuffed two fingers inside her as she moaned. She opened her legs wider, so my fingers were able to get inside deeper. Right before I was about to haul her off to the bedroom, there was a knock at the door.

"Whoever it is, get rid of them!" I ordered. She nodded her head and went to answer the door.

"Are you okay? OMG!! O'Shea did that, didn't he?" Felicia asked as she pushed her way inside the apartment. "How many times do I have to tell you that he ain't no good for you?"

I heard the door close as Sassy walked back to the living room. I could hear Felicia still running her mouth. That bitch was always sticking her nose where it didn't belong. When she rounded the corner and saw me, her face hit the floor. She turned to Sassy for answers.

"What is he doing here? After what he did to you, why would you let him in?"

I walked up to Felicia and backhanded the shit out of her. I slapped that bitch so hard that she lost her balance and fell to the floor. As she struggled to get her bearings, I towered over her.

"Did she tell you I did that to her? You too fuckin' nosey and always making mess! Comin' up in here stickin' ya fuckin' nose where it don't belong and shit!" I yelled.

"Muthafucka you got me fucked up! Don't you ever put your muthafuckin' hands on me again!" Felicia shouted as she rubbed her cheek that had already turned a crimson shade of red.

I grabbed her by the hair. "Or what bitch? What the fuck you gon' do about it?"

She tried to get me to turn her loose, but I was too strong. "Rhianna help me! Call 911!" she cried.

Sassy just stood and watched. It was almost like she was in a trance or something. "Sassy get over here baby!" She quickly rushed to my side as I stuck my tongue down her throat again. A moan escaped from her lips as I stared at Felicia's dumb ass. "Now what bitch!"

Felicia began to cry like a baby at that point. "I'm sorry O'Shea! You're right, I stuck my nose in your business and assumed something I shouldn't have. If you let me go, I won't say anything to anyone! I promise!" she begged.

"Well, that ain't gonna happen," I responded with a sinister smile. "But since you're willing to do anything, let's move this party to the bedroom?"

I twisted Felicia's arm behind her back as she winced in pain. Sassy followed me to her bedroom. Felicia continued to cry and beg to be let go. She was even begging Sassy for her help, almost as if she didn't understand where her loyalties lied. Once inside Sassy's bedroom, I punched Felicia in her stomach. I needed her to know who the fuck was in charge. As she whined on the floor, I heard Sassy trying to calm her down.

"Felicia, just stop fighting him and maybe he won't hurt you too bad," Sassy told her.

I grabbed her up from off the floor. "Here's how this is gonna work... I'll tell you what to do and you'll do as I say. If I'm satisfied by the end of the night, I'll let you go. But if I'm not satisfied, I'll kill you. If I let you go and you go to the cops, I promise you won't live to see your trial take place. Are we clear? Sassy that goes for you too, babe and you know I'm not joking!"

They both nodded their heads in understanding.

"Try and relax ladies because this is going to be a long night!" I informed them with a devilish grin.

Chapter seven

Noelle

One week later...

Things between Zach and I had been going so good it was almost like a dream come true. How did I get so lucky to have such a special man in my life? I mean, to have to deal with O'Shea who was just the absolute worst. And now to have Zach... it was like a gift from God himself. Zach was loving, hardworking, attentive, and an excellent support system. We had started exercising together, and he showered me with praise all the time. I never had a man support me this much. It was crazy, but it felt damn good.

He mentioned to me that O'Shea had called that day, but I didn't care. Whatever mess he had gotten himself into was his business and his alone. I was living my best life with Zach. As we sat in the living room of his apartment watching television, he turned to me.

"What?" I asked.

"I feel like the luckiest man alive."

"Really?"

"Hell yea! You don't realize how great a woman you are," he said.

"It's taken me a while to understand what a catch I really am, but I finally know my worth." That was true. Had I never gotten involved with Zach, O'Shea would probably still be using and abusing me. When I think back to all the shit he put me through, I cringe.

I couldn't believe how weak I was for that loser. To be involved in a threesome and lick another bitch's kitty cat...UGH! If he had any respect for me, he would've never treated me that way. But that was the problem, he had no respect for me. He had me do things I never would've done if I had been in my right frame of mind. At that time, I was in a low place with very low self-esteem. I even thought that I was in love with him.

Now that I had met Zach, he had shown me how worthy I was. He had shown me a different kind of man and I was deep in love with him. That man made me feel so special and loved. "You've always been worthy bae. You were just with the wrong man," he said as he gazed into my eyes. He lifted my chin with his finger and kissed my lips. "But you got the right one now."

"Thanks for being so patient with me," I said.

"No thanks needed babe. Anything worth having is worth the work. You are a wonderful woman, and I pray for you every single night."

"I pray for you too, Zach."

"Then we already have the right tools to form a solid foundation. A family that prays together stays together," he said.

"You're right about that."

"I never thought I'd fall for you this fast. You are such an incredible woman," he said.

"Where have you been all my life?"

I was truly lucky and blessed to have him.

"I've been looking for you," he said as he kissed me.

The two of us made our way to the bedroom where we made sweet love all night long. I had no idea sex with the right person could be this good. I had given my virginity to the wrong man, but I'd never make that mistake again. Now that I had Zach in my life, the only way he'd ever get rid of me was if he decided he didn't want to be with me anymore. He was someone I saw myself growing old with.

Ladies, when you find a man who can uplift your entire spirit... I mean, eat, pray, and love you... keep him. Zach and I met at one of the lowest points of my life. I believe God sent him to me for the sole purpose of getting me out of O'Shea's clutches.

When O'Shea and I were together, I thought I deserved to be treated that way. I had never had a man in my life before, so who was I gonna compare him to? When I think back, I didn't know how I even fell for him. But then I listened to Zach when he said that O'Shea took advantage of me and my inexperience and used it to his advantage. What a sorry excuse for a man... to treat women like they're undeserving of love.

As Zach slowly rotated his hips against mine, I crooned at the orgasm that was rushing to escape my body. I felt it flowing from my soul, and as it traveled to the edge of my tunnel, my body shook. I grabbed Zach's face and kissed him at the exact moment I gushed against him. He drove his tongue in my mouth and they swirled and swirled until he reached his own climax.

Afterward, I laid in his arms as he talked about our future. I was actually surprised to hear him mention a future with me. Not that I wasn't happy. I knew he said he loved me, but I guess I never realized how much.

"You see a future with me?" I asked as I gazed into his eyes with my chin against his chest.

"Yes. Why? Don't you see yourself with me in the future?" he asked, a serious expression on his handsome face.

"I can see myself growing old with you. I just didn't think you felt that way."

"Noelle, if it seems as if I'm hard to read, it's not because I'm trying to be that way. It's just, after everything you've been through, I don't ever want to rush or push you. I just want to move at a pace that's comfortable for you because you're worth the wait."

"That's the sweetest thing anyone has ever said to me," I said as a tear slipped from my eye. He brushed it away and kissed me.

"I promise that you'll never be treated as anything but what you are... a queen."

Oh my God! How did I get so lucky?

The next day, I was meeting Wynter, Brandie and one of her friends from school, Felicia. I took one look at Felicia and knew that she was a dancer. Her long blond weave, long acrylic fingernails, big bouncy booty, and those eyelashes were so long they curled upward. But she was still beautiful all the same. As the three of us sat in the front portion of the bridal salon sipping champagne, Wynter tried on dresses.

As I side-eyed Felicia, I could see signs of abuse. She had used makeup to cover up a bruise on her right cheek, but I could still see it. Whoever had hit her had meant to do some damage. She also wore a turtleneck with long sleeves and it wasn't even cold. We were in Florida and the temperature was 72 degrees. Something definitely wasn't right.

"Felicia, you strip right?" Brandie asked. She was never one to hold her tongue for anything. I mean, I had the same thought but wasn't going to say anything to the woman.

"I prefer dancer, so in answer to your question, the answer is yes. Why is that important? Have you seen me dance before or something?" Felicia asked. It was clear that she had an attitude.

"Oh, I didn't mean to offend you or anything like that..." Brandie said.

"Trust me, I'm not offended. I get asked that question all the time."

"I can imagine," Brandie said. "You are fine as fuck!"

I knew Brandie had experimented with females before, but she had a man now. I just hoped she wasn't trying to get into something with this female. There was something about her that just didn't sit right with me.

She blushed as she responded, "Thank you."

"So, how long you been knowing Wynter?"

"We met last year during spring semester. We had a couple of the same classes," Felicia said.

"Yea, that's right. She did say that you were in college. Do strippers... I mean, dancers need a college education these days?" Brandie asked.

Brandie was a straight fool for asking that question. Before Felicia could answer, Wynter walked out in her first dress. It was a strapless mermaid style with feathers at the bottom and a long train. The details on the gown were so exquisite. She looked absolutely beautiful.

"Oh my God! You look amazing!" I gushed as I stared at my childhood best friend. I was so happy for her and Tripp.

"Yea girl, you look beautiful!" Brandie said.

"You are really outshining the dress, and that dress is beautiful!" Felicia said.

What kind of shit was that to say? Just say she was beautiful and be done with it.

"Y'all really like it?" Wynter asked as she stared at herself in the full-length mirror.

"It's not about whether we really like it. It's about you and how you feel in it," Felicia said.

"I feel beautiful!"

"You look beautiful!" Felicia said.

"I don't think you should settle on the first dress though. I think you should try on a few more. On that show, *Say Yes to the Dress*, they always say to try more than one dress before you make a decision," I said.

"So, you've been watching *Say Yes to the Dress* huh? Is there something that we should know?" Brandie asked.

"No. Well, Zach hasn't proposed yet or anything, but last night while we lay in bed, he said he saw a future with me," I admitted.

"Aw, Noelle, that's great! I could see the two of you getting married too," Wynter said.

"Yea, he's a way better catch for you than that triflin' ass O'Shea!" Brandie said.

"Anybody would've been better than O'Shea's crazy ass," Wynter said.

"I don't wanna talk about him. He's a thing of the past, and Zach is my future," I said.

"You're right! Let's not ruin this perfect day by talking about some worthless piece of shit!" Brandie said.

"Wynter you look amazing, but go try on another one," I said with a smile.

She smiled and rushed off to try on another dress. As we sat back down to wait for her, I noticed how quiet Felicia had gotten. She actually had turned white, almost as if she had seen a ghost.

"You alright girl?" I asked as I touched her arm.

"DON'T TOUCH ME!" she said as she jumped up.

"I'm sorry. I was just..." Tears began to fall from her eyes. "Are you okay?"

"I gotta go! Tell Wynter I'll call her later," she said as she grabbed her purse and flew out the door.

"Shit, I wonder what the fuck wrong with her ass," Brandie said.

"Me too."

I didn't really know Felicia, but I was concerned about her. Something happened to that girl and I could tell because of her reaction when I touched her arm. She had been abused by somebody and I recognized the signs. I used to act the same way when I was dating O'Shea's ass. I prayed that she was able to get away from the man that had caused her to react that way.

When Wynter came back out in another dress, she looked around for her friend.

"Where's Felicia?" she asked.

"She said she had to go and would call you later," I said.

"Just like that. What happened? Brandie, did you say something to her?"

"No, I didn't do anything to that girl, but somebody did," Brandie said.

"What do you mean?" Wynter asked.

"She was crying and shit and just ran out of her like a bat outta hell! Something wrong with yo friend!"

"This is a conversation we should be having at another time. You look absolutely beautiful in that dress! You look like Cinderella!" I said.

She was now wearing an off the shoulder ball gown with a tulle train and a lot of beading. It was a way different look than the first gown she tried on. "You don't think it's too much?" she asked.

"Hell yea, it's too much!" Brandie said. "But it's for your wedding day. Everything is supposed to be over the top, right?"

"Right," Wynter said as she looked at herself in the mirror. "I don't like this one as much as I like the first one though."

"Then try another one," I said.

"Will do," she said and walked back to the dressing room.

She tried on about seven more dresses before she put the first one back on. The sales woman who had been helping her put a blinged out ribbon around her waist and a veil on her head. Wynter had tears in her eyes when she looked at herself in the mirror. Her reaction was just like those other women from the show.

I hoped when it was my turn, I'd be as beautiful as her.

Chapter eight

Sassy

Last night was one of the most horrible nights of my life. I had to watch O'Shea abuse my friend, and I couldn't do anything about it. It was like I wanted to say something, but the words wouldn't come. I wanted to call the police, but I couldn't. As a matter of fact, I had gone down to the police station earlier today and dropped the charges against him. I knew I shouldn't have done that, but it was like he had me under his spell. I didn't know if he had voodoo on me or what, but I wouldn't put it past him.

O'Shea loved being in control of his women. I wish I could get away from him as easily as Felicia. She was able to go home and take a hot bath. I was still in the apartment with him. As I stared at the bite marks on my neck and chest, a tear slipped from my eye. I quickly brushed it away because if O'Shea had caught me crying, I don't know what he would've done.

I had never been so out of control because of a man as I was with O'Shea. It was like I was losing my identity and couldn't do shit about it. I knew that I had lost my best friend after last night. I tried texting her a few times, but they all went unanswered. I couldn't call her because I knew O'Shea would be pissed. I just hoped she knew last night was just outta my hands.

O'Shea came up behind me and asked, "Whatchu in here thinking bout?"

"Nothing really."

"You can be honest with me."

"I was just wondering if these bite marks will ever go away. I dance for a living Shea. Who's gonna wanna pay me with these marks on my neck and chest like that?" I asked as I stared at him in the mirror.

"Are you kidding? You can cover that shit with some makeup! Those niggas at the strip club ain't coming to look at nothing but your ass and pussy!"

"I guess," I said as I released a sigh.

O'Shea could be such an ass. I wished I had the strength to tell him how I really feel. I wanted him out of my life so bad but didn't know how to get rid of him.

"Come suck my dick. It'll make you feel better."

Yea right! He meant it would make him feel better. Sucking his dick didn't do shit for me. So why was I getting down on my knees to suck his dick though? That's the shit I was talking about. I hated O'Shea, but it was like I had no control over my feelings or anything. As I reached for his dick, I massaged it slowly the way he liked. Then I rolled my tongue around his beefy head before taking it in my mouth.

As I flexed my throat to accommodate the girth of his dick, I sucked. He leaned against the bathroom counter as I went to work. He held my head in place and fucked my mouth until I gagged. He pulled me up roughly and leaned me over the counter, pushed my panties to the side and slammed into me from behind. As he stroked my clit, he fucked me hard.

He fucked me hard as he whispered in my ear that I belonged to him. Then he turned my head and kissed me hard on the lips. I moaned as he held my hair in his hands while watching me from behind in the mirror.

"You love that dick?"

"Yes," I said.

I wasn't lying. I did love his dick. I just hated him and wanted him dead. I was going to have to find a way to get rid of this man though. He was no good for me or any other woman for that matter. He was evil and had to be dealt with.

For the next six weeks, everything continued to go O'Shea's way. I was just glad that he wasn't beating me anymore. He was actually treating me pretty good. It was almost as if we were in an exclusive relationship with each other. We were out driving down the boulevard one day when we spotted a man and woman coming out of Quizno's. His mood changed almost immediately. Whereas a couple of minutes ago, he was smiling, laughing and singing songs from his Bluetooth, he now sat with his lip poked out. I could tell from the way he was gripping the steering wheel that he was angry.

"Who is that?" I asked.

"Just some bitch."

"Just some bitch huh?"

"That's what the fuck I said," he responded angrily.

I grabbed a hold of his hand in an attempt to calm him down. For a minute, it looked like it was working. But then the guy leaned in and kissed the female before he opened her car door for her. Suddenly, he was squeezing my hand so hard, I cried out in pain.

"Who is that? Why are you so upset?" I asked.

"That's the bitch who thought her fat ass was too good for me!" he fumed.

Fat? Well, sure she was a little thick, but she wasn't fat. It made me wonder if we were even looking at the same female.

"Well, you don't need her anymore. You have me," I said.

WHAP!

"Shut the fuck up!!" he said through clenched teeth. "You don't know shit about her or what we had!"

He fumed the whole way to Home Depot. I didn't know what we were doing here because this wasn't on our list of things to do at all.

"What are we doing here?" I asked.

"Don't you know me well enough to know not to question me?"

"Sorry," I said as we got out the car. I followed him inside quietly.

I watched as he purchased duct tape, rope, trash bags and pliers. I wondered what he planned to do with those things, but didn't question him. Once he paid for the items we got back in the car and drove to his place in silence.

Once at the condo, he turned to me with a weird smile on his face.

"Sassy you know I love you right?"

What? He loved me? Where the hell did that come from? Of course, I didn't believe him one bit because if he really did love me, he'd refer to me by my given name instead of my stripper name. However, if I wanted to know what he was up to, I had to play nice.

"Yea, I know," I lied.

"I need your help with something," he said.

"Anything," I responded without hesitation.

"I need you to help me put these bitches in their place."

"I don't understand what you mean."

"Noelle, Felicia, Tamika, and her bitch ass sister Ava. All of them ho's need to be taught a lesson and I need you to help me. Are you willing to do that?"

"I don't know what you mean. How are you going to teach them a lesson?" I asked.

"We'll discuss all that later. I just need to know if you riding for a nigga," he asked.

"Yea."

As always, his dick was hard, so he pulled it out and began to stroke it. As he stared into my eyes, he said, "That's good. Now, I need you to undress and come over here so daddy can put this big dick in you!"

I did as I was told because as I said, O'Shea has some real good dick. I knelt before him and took his dick in my mouth. I let him fuck my mouth and this time I didn't gag. When his dick was soaking wet, he lifted me up off the floor with my dripping wet pussy dangling over his dick and shoved it inside my soft box. He fucked me while holding me in the air with my legs wrapped around his waist. He held my hips and guided my pussy up and down, making sure to hit deep and touching my G-spot.

I shivered and shuddered with pleasure as he kissed me deeply. He asked me to turn around, so I did. He positioned himself behind me and pumped into me real hard. After several minutes, he pulled out of me and said, "You know what time it is right?"

I already knew what he wanted. I opened the drawer and grabbed the lubrication. He wanted to fuck me in the ass and even though I wasn't fond of that position, I had gotten used to it. As long as he used the lubrication, I didn't mind. He poured some on my ass and massaged it in. Then he poured some on his dick and slid it into my anus.

I must have done something right because he moved in and out of me slowly. He wasn't trying to hurt me too much, thank God. He wrapped a hand around my throat and applied a little pressure. As I turned my face to his, he inserted his tongue in my mouth. After about 30 minutes or so, he finally released all over my big yellow ass. He grabbed me by the hair and kissed me passionately. Our sex session continued for the next three hours. By the time we were done, I was so tired.

All I wanted to do was sleep. Unfortunately, O'Shea had other plans. He wanted to talk, and the shit he was talking about had my mind reeling.

Chapter nine

O'Shea

"So, you understand what we gotta do?" I asked as I stroked her hair.

"Not really."

"Sassy, I really need you to be on board with this shit."

"But I don't understand what you want me to do," she said.

I rolled my eyes upward. I couldn't believe that she still didn't understand what I wanted her to do. I needed her to do this for me. I needed her to do this with me.

"O'Shea do you love me? I mean, like do you really love me?" she asked.

"Yes, I love you. You're my rider. That's why I want you to do this with me because it's something we can share. It's some shit that will bring us closer together. Don't you want us to be closer?" I asked.

"Of course, I just have a bad feeling about whatever this is that you want us to do. Aren't I enough woman for you? Don't I make you happy?" she asked.

No woman could make me happy. The woman I really wanted didn't want me. She had moved on with some other nigga. She had lost weight and was looking good as fuck. I didn't know what the hell Noelle saw in that lil dorky ass dude. I mean, what the fuck could he do for her that I couldn't do?

I didn't wanna fight with Sassy. She was my girl now, and I wanted us to move on with this pain. If she did this with me, she wouldn't have to worry about no other bitch taking her attention from me. It would be just me and her.

"Babe I already explained why I have to do this!"

"But you didn't though. You just said you wanted to get back at those women. Why though? Why can't we just let them be happy? Why can't I make you happy enough to forget about them?"

"Look babe, this is gonna go down whether you want it to or not. You're either with me or against me... it's totally up to you. But if you're against me, you already know what will happen to you for going against the grain," I said as I stared her down. "So, here's how it's gonna go down... we are going to take Ava..."

"Take Ava? What do you mean take Ava?" she asked.

It was taking everything I had in me not to hit her. It was like she was stuck on stupid or something. "I mean, we're gonna kidnap the bitch! Once we have her, then we'll grab Felicia. They will be the easiest ones to take.

We'll bring them here, handcuff them, then go get the other two women. Do you understand now?"

"But what are we going to do with them once we get them here?"

"We're going to do what we did to Felicia, except this time they won't go home," I said.

"What do you mean they won't go home?" she asked, confusion written all over her face.

"WE ARE GOING TO KILL THE BITCHES!! GOTDAMN YO ASS IS SLOW!!" I shouted.

"Oh my God! Kill them? I didn't know you wanted to kill anyone."

"What the fuck you thought I was gonna do with them... play cards?"

"No, but Shea, I'm not a killer and neither are you. We can't do this!" she said.

"What the fuck you mean we can't do this? We can do it and we will," I said.

"I-I-I can't be a part of this. You can't do this! Felicia is my best friend. You want me to kill my best friend?"

"Yes! Fuckin' right!"

"But why?"

"Because those women crossed me! Gotdammit, didn't I tell you that before!"

"You're gonna have to kill me then because I can't do this," she cried as she hopped out of the bed.

Why was she doing this? Surely, she thought this was a joke. Otherwise, she'd just do what I asked her to do. Before I could get her ass, she rushed in the bathroom, shut the door and locked it.

"SASSY! OPEN THE DOOR SASSY!" I yelled from outside the door. "SASSY, DON'T MAKE ME BREAK THIS FUCKIN' DOOR DOWN!!"

I couldn't hear shit in that bathroom, so it had me wondering what the fuck she was doing in there. "OPEN THE FUCKIN' DOOR!!" I yelled again. When she didn't open the door, I began pounding it with my shoulder in an attempt to break it down. After several attempts, I remembered the little key to open it. I rushed to the dresser drawer and retrieved the key. "I'M ABOUT TO FUCK YOU UP!!"

I used the key and finally got the door open, only to find the bathroom empty and the window open. "DAMMIT!!" I yelled as I rushed through the apartment to get to the front door. I opened the door and scanned the parking lot looking for Sassy. I didn't see her anywhere. Her car was still in the parking lot, so I didn't know where she would go without it. She didn't have her phone, keys, or nothing.

I went back inside the apartment. I prayed that she wasn't going to do anything stupid, like tell those bitches what I had planned or the police. But this was some straight bullshit because I couldn't pull this shit off without her.

This was why I couldn't be in a relationship. Women just didn't listen when I told them to do something. I remember the lessons my dad taught me when I was younger. He said that women were put on this earth to obey their men. They were supposed to be submissive to men at all times. I used to have control over all my women, but somehow they had decided to have minds of their own. I needed to show them that I was the boss and they couldn't just cross me and not suffer the consequences.

But how could I do any of that without Sassy's help? Dammit! She had really fucked everything up. I walked in the room and got dressed. I was gonna go get that ungrateful bitch and bring her back here. She was ungrateful because I gave her a fucking pass to live and she betrayed me. I could've put her on that list, but I didn't. I grabbed my keys and was heading for the door when I heard knocking.

I bet that was her coming back for her keys and phone. I rushed to the door and pulled it back to find my dad standing there with a frown on his face.

"Hey dad," I greeted.

"Hey dad huh? No hug, no nothing huh?"

"Sorry dad," I said as I hugged him. "I'm just shocked to see you. What are you doing here?" I asked as he walked in.

"Well, I figured since you out there getting yourself locked up and shit, I needed to come see what the hell going on with you."

What the fuck? How the hell did my dad know that I had been in jail? I certainly hadn't told him. "What?"

"You heard me boy! Don't act like yo ass is deaf or something!"

"Who told you that I was in jail?"

He smirked and looked at me as if I had lost my mind. "Fuck all that! Why haven't I heard from you since you got released? You couldn't even thank me for bailing yo ass out?"

"What? You bailed me out?" I asked. I hadn't checked to see who bailed me out. Shit, at the time I didn't care. I was just happy to be out.

"Yes! I bailed you out and yo ass didn't even have the decency to call and say thanks."

"I'm sorry dad. I didn't know it was you that bailed me out."

"You didn't know it was me? Who did you think it was... the bail fairies?" he asked in a condescending tone.

"I'm sorry dad."

"So, what were you in jail for?"

"A misunderstanding," I said.

"A misunderstanding huh? I was told you raped somebody," he said.

"What? Nah, I ain't raped nobody. As a matter of fact, she dropped the charges because like I said, it was a misunderstanding."

"I know I didn't raise you to be no rapist. My son don't need to rape no woman!"

"I know dad, and I didn't. That's why she dropped the charges."

"Well, here my keys. Go get my bags out the car!" he said as he tossed me his car keys.

"Bags? How long you plan on staying?" I asked.

How could my dad think it was okay to just show up to my place uninvited and unannounced and think it was all good.

"I plan on staying at least a week. I'm on vacation from my job, so I ain't got no reason to rush home."

A week? My dad was gonna be here for a whole week? What the hell was I gonna do with him for a whole week?

"Don't just stand there, son. Go get my damn bags!"

I headed out the door and went to get his bags. Who the hell had told my dad I got arrested? Having him here was gonna fuck up everything I had planned. I was gonna have to find a way to get him outta here sooner rather than later. There was no way he was staying here for no damn week.

The next morning, I was brewing coffee for me and my dad when there was a knock at the door. It was only ten in the morning, so I wondered who could be at my damn door. I knew it wasn't the police because they'd be knocking way louder. I pulled the door open and there stood Sassy and Felicia. Damn. I couldn't have asked for a better way to start my day than with a threesome. I smiled at them, but they weren't smiling back with me.

"Can I have my car keys and phone please?" Sassy asked as the two of them barged in.

"What?"

I was confused. Surely, the two of them didn't come here looking and smelling all good just to get some car keys and a fucking phone. "I came to get my keys and phone," Sassy repeated.

"Shit, I thought y'all came by for some dick," I smirked.

"Hell no! Don't nobody want that ol' nasty dick!" Felicia said with a grimace.

See... that right there was the reason I wanted to kill her ass. The blatant disrespect was driving me crazy. I looked at Sassy for her to say something to her friend, but she just stood there. I should've smacked the shit out of both of them.

"Sassy, you just gon' let her disrespect me like that?" I asked.

"O'Shea, all I want are my keys and my phone. I don't want any trouble from you. After I get my shit, you won't ever hear from me again and I never wanna hear from you again either," Sassy said.

"That's how it is? You just gon' come in here with this bitch and disrespect me in my own house!" I fumed.

"I'm not trying to disrespect you and you just disrespected us by calling us bitches," Sassy responded.

"I didn't call you a bitch. I called her a bitch!"

"You're the bitch!" Felicia said. "And you're a sick one too!"

"Bitch I will beat the fuck out yo ass!" I said.

"Do it and I'll go straight to the police! I'm sick and tired of your shit O'Shea! You need help!" Felicia said.

I yoked her up against the wall by her neck and growled in her face. "Bitch you got a lot of fuckin' nerve coming in my house with that shit!"

"O'Shea let her go!" Sassy yelled as she tried to get me to let Felicia go. That bitch had a lot to say two minutes ago, but she ain't had shit to say now.

I pushed Sassy off me. "Get the fuck off me!" I said.

"WHAT THE HELL IS GOING ON IN HERE?!!" my dad asked.

I quickly released Felicia and she began gasping for air.

"O'Shea, I asked you a question son. What the hell is going on here?"

"Nothing dad. I got everything under control," I said.

"You got everything under control? You were choking that woman! That is hardly the attitude of someone who has shit under control!" my dad said.

"Mr. Washington, my name is Rhianna, and this is my friend Felicia. Your son and I got in a huge argument last night and I ended up leaving without my phone and car keys. That's all I came by to get and I'll be out of here," Sassy said.

"Do you know where your things are?" he asked.

"Yes sir, they're on the nightstand in the bedroom."

"O'Shea I want you to go get this young lady's shit!"

"Dad you don't..."

"Don't back talk me boy! Just do what the fuck I told you to do!" he fumed.

Who the fuck did my dad think he was talking to like that? I was a grown ass man! I wasn't the same little kid he scared with the sound of his voice back in the day.

"Did you hear what I said?" he asked.

I walked off to go get the keys and phone. I was pissed because he had insinuated himself in some shit that had nothing to do with him. This was none of his business, so why was he getting involved in my shit? I marched back to the front room and handed Sassy her shit.

"Thank you," she said to me. "Nice to meet you Mr. Washington."

She and Felicia began walking toward the door. "Sassy you just gonna leave like that?"

She stopped and turned around to look at me. "My name is Rhianna! You claim you love me, but you still can't call me by my damn name!" she said with tears in her eyes.

What the fuck was she crying about? This whole thing was straight bullshit!

"I do love you girl! Stop playin'!"

"Love? LOVE?!" she laughed as tears streamed from her eyes. Was she having a nervous breakdown or something? No one laughs and cries at the same time. "You don't know what love is! Love doesn't leave marks like this on you! Love doesn't hurt the way you've hurt me! You need help O'Shea before you kill someone. And to make sure that someone isn't going to be me, I never wanna see you again!"

"You did that to her?" my dad asked.

"Dad..."

"Don't dad me! You left those bite marks on this young woman?"

"These young women," Felicia corrected as she showed her marks. These bitches were really ruining my fucking life.

"Oh my God! Ladies, I am going to apologize to you for my son's behavior. I can assure you that he will get the help he needs, and he won't bother you again," my dad said.

Shit, I don't need help and he shouldn't be making promises for me that he had no control over. That nigga was fucked up for that shit.

"Thank you Mr. Washington. Your son really needs some serious help," Felicia said.

The two of them walked out, leaving me to deal with my dad. "What the hell is wrong with you boy? Have you lost your fucking mind?"

"Whatchu mean? I'm only doing what you taught me to do!"

"Now that's a damn lie! I never told you to choke and bite women!"

"You told me to keep my women under control and that they had to be submissive to me, like mom was to you."

"Boy, you are losing your mind! Your mother was submissive meaning she washed my clothes, ironed them, cooked, and cleaned. But she would've never put up with no shit like what you were doing to those females. Are you trying to go to jail for the rest of your life?"

"You told me to stay in control!"

"Stay in control is a mind thing, not a hand thing. You ain't got to hit or beat up on a woman to control them!" he said. "Both of those women said you raped them!"

"What? I ain't never raped no one and I resent you for coming at me like that! You're my father, so you're supposed to be on my side!" I said.

"I'm on your side as long as you're doing the right thing. When you start doing shit like this, I can't be on your side!"

"What's that supposed to mean?"

"Have you ever seen me raise a hand to your mother? Shit, your mom, God rest her soul, would've had me hemmed up by the neck if I had! I didn't raise you this way son. Those females are right... you do need help!"

"I don't need no help! I'm good, trust and believe that!"

"You ain't good! What the hell would've happened if I hadn't walked in when I did? Would you have killed that woman? Because you could've," he said.

Now, my dad was really making more out of this than it was. I wouldn't have killed Felicia. I was just teaching her a quick lesson about respect.

"I wasn't gonna kill that girl!"

"How do you know that? When you released her, she was gasping for air. That type of behavior ain't normal," he said.

"Dad you are really making too much out of this," I said.

"And you aren't making a big enough of a deal. You are acting like that shit is okay. It ain't okay! You need help son."

"I don't need help, so I wish you'd stop telling me that shit!"

"You better watch your damn tone and how you speak to me! You ain't too grown for me to whoop your ass!" he said.

Unfortunately, he continued the conversation for the rest of the day. Lord help me!

Chapter ten

Wynter

Since I had moved in with Tripp, I didn't get to spend as much time with my girls as I would've liked. It wasn't even just because of the move. I had been really busy planning the wedding, which was taking place in just three months. Brandie and Noelle were very understanding though, most likely because they had their own relationships to tend to.

But I decided to host a brunch for our mothers and my bridesmaids... just so I could thank them for everything they had been doing to help me pull this wedding together. I had made reservations for 11:30 at 94th Aero Squadron Restaurant. We were all going to meet there. My parents were paying for the wedding, so it was turning out to be a bigger event than I had planned. After finalizing the guest list, the RSVP count was at 380.

I was so happy for my girls too. Noelle had found an amazing man in Zach. He helped her see how truly beautiful she was. She had insecurities with her weight, so with his help she now ate healthier and exercised on a regular basis. I was extremely proud of her and happy that she was happy. Zach was a different kind of dude... he was a man and that was exactly what Noelle needed after dealing with a nigga like O'Shea.

Zach was easy to get along with. He listened to her, was very attentive and according to her, he knew how to express his feelings easily. That was good because she never had to wonder or guess how he felt about anything. He also showered her with little gifts and trinkets to let her know how much he cared about her. Zach was truly one in a million.

But he wasn't better than my man though. Tripp was the absolute best. I had never known that life with a man could be so good. He wanted to pay for the wedding, but my parents insisted. They said that the parents of the bride were supposed to pay, and they wouldn't have it any other way. Tripp was surprising me with our honeymoon though. I didn't know where we were going at all. He told me not to worry about it, so I'm leaving it in his hands.

As I stared at my reflection in the bathroom mirror, I looked great. My makeup and hair were on point, my eyebrows and lashes slayed and my outfit was off the chain. I wore a white lace mini dress with a plunging neckline by Alexis Parisa. The belt was in the form of a silver zipper. It was very beautiful.

On my feet, I wore a silver pair of Giuseppe Zanotti lace up sandals. I was proud with the way that I looked.

"What time are you meeting the women at the restaurant?" he asked.

"11:30. I told you that last night babe," I said as I put my earring in my ear.

"I know." He looked at his watch then back at me.

"Why? Do you have somewhere you need to be?"

He walked over to me as he licked his lips. I held up my hand and backed up. "Uh uh, you are not gonna make me late for an event that I planned," I said with a smile.

"You won't be late babe. It's 10:00, you'll be there in plenty of time," he said.

"Babe, I have to drive 45 minutes to get there... on a Sunday. There's gonna be a lot of church traffic," I argued as he lifted the skirt of my dress.

"Your skin is so soft," he said as he massaged my inner thighs while kissing my neck.

"Babe, we can't..." I said as his lips landed on mine. As we shared a heated kiss, he lifted me up onto the bathroom counter and spread my legs. "Mmmm."

He slid my silk thong over and then pressed against me. I felt the head of his dick as it teased my awaiting kitty. "You ready?" he whispered.

"Always ready for you baby," I crooned.

"Ohhh shit!" I moaned as he entered me. We both looked down and watched as his dick went in and out of my kitty. I didn't know how bad I wanted him until I saw my cream on his dick. I bit down on my bottom lip as he smiled.

He kissed me hungrily as he went deeper inside me. He lifted me off the counter and held my small frame in his hands as he guided me up and down his shaft. "I love you," he whispered huskily in my ear as he nibbled on it.

"I love you," I whispered back as I sucked his shoulder.

Because of the business that Tripp was in, I never left my love marks on his neck. I always left them on his chest or his shoulder. He was a professional and I respected that. And I only sucked on him when he pounded too hard. Instead of screaming like a banshee, I sucked.

As my orgasm built to the surface, I shuddered against him. He held me close as we released at the same time. He kissed me before planting my feet on the bathroom rug. My knees shook like blades of grass in the wind as I tried to steady my balance. I grabbed a washcloth and applied soap to the towel.

"We could just jump in the shower real quick," he said with a smile.

"I don't have time," I said as I rubbed the soapy towel between my legs. I rinsed myself off and slipped my panties back on.

"So, you just gonna run out on me like that?" Tripp asked as he stood in the bathroom doorway with his pants down to his ankles.

"Yep. See you later babe."

"Tell my mom and sister I said hello!"

"I will," I said as I grabbed my keys and my Prada saffino clutch.

I was looking forward to seeing the ladies today. My mom, Tripp's mom, his sister and my bridesmaids would be joining me this morning. Tripp's sister was also in my wedding. She was only 18, but I wanted her to be a part of our big day. As I slid into the driver's seat of my BMW, I started the car. The engine purred to life and the smooth sounds of Chris Brown bellowed through the speakers.

I backed out of the garage and headed down the highway. Thank God there wasn't too much traffic, so I made it to the location in less than an hour. After I parked my car, I headed inside. As I strutted toward the door, I pulled my skirt down because I didn't want my ass showing.

I walked in and the hostess immediately walked over to me. The scent of my perfume tickled my own nose as

I smiled with her. "Good morning, table for one?" she asked.

"No, I'm actually having a brunch here today. I'm expecting about 10 other guests," I explained.

"Oh, yes. Let me show you to your table."

I followed behind her while some of the customers stared at me as I walked by. It wasn't their fault though. My presence exuded attention, they couldn't help but look. When I got to the table, my mom, Brandie and Noelle were already there. I hugged and greeted them all and sat down at the head of the table. The other women began to file in a short time later and we commenced to celebrating my appreciation for them.

We had a great time and three hours later, we left the restaurant. I hugged everyone and was getting into my car when I heard someone call my name. I turned and was surprised to see Lewis, an ex I hadn't seen in over three years. My heart plummeted as soon as he smiled. Lewis was the last person I expected or wanted to see out here.

"I thought that was you and your mom," he said as he approached me. He reached in for a hug, so I gave him one. What else could I do? My body trembled and I cringed at his touch, but I was trying to keep my cool.

Lewis was my first boyfriend and worse nightmare in high school. I thought I had left him back home, but I guess I hadn't. "Hey Lewis, how are you?" I asked.

"Great! Hell, I'm even better now that I found you. How are you?" he asked as he licked his lips. "You're even more beautiful than I remembered."

Found me? Had he been searching for me? Had he been stalking me... AGAIN?!

"Thanks, I'm fantastic!" I blushed as I tucked my hair behind my ear. "What are you doing out here in Miami?"

"You didn't hear the news?"

"What news?"

"I moved out here to open a nightclub a couple of months ago."

"Wow! I didn't know you were in the nightclub business," I said.

"I'm in any business that makes me money," he said with a smile.

"I had no idea you were thinking about moving to Miami."

"Well, actually I wasn't until I came down here for vacation and got a feel of the nightlife. After that, I was hooked. You live in Miami, right?"

"Yes. Me, Brandie and Noelle moved here right after graduation."

Of course, he already knew that because I had told everyone in our senior class that the girls and I were moving to Miami. Lewis and I had broken up during our senior year. I had caught him cheating with Amanda's grimy ass and ended it immediately. Lewis, however, had a hard time letting things end. He practically stalked me the last few months before graduation. When I thought I couldn't take it anymore, he finally stopped.

I was finally able to breathe and be myself again... until now.

"Oh yea! I had forgotten all about that," he said.

I didn't believe that shit for one minute. I wouldn't be surprised if he had been watching me and that was how we ended up in the same place today.

"Well, it was nice seeing you again, but I really have to get going."

"Maybe we can do lunch some time," he offered.

"I'd like to Lewis, but I've been so busy lately. I'm getting married in three months, so I wouldn't have the time to join you for lunch," I declined.

"Oh wow! You're getting married huh?" I could see the tensed look in his face and the tightness of his jawbone. Yea, this little meeting wasn't by chance at all.

"Yes, but I gotta go. Take care." I opened my door and hurriedly slid my ass behind the wheel. I started the car and drove off, quick, fast and in a fucking hurry.

I saw Lewis watching me as I drove out of the parking lot. That shit was really creepy. I immediately called Noelle and Brandie on a three-way call. There was no way that I could keep this shit to myself.

"Hey girl," Brandie answered.

"Hey Wynter. We just left you. Did you forget to tell us something?" Noelle asked.

"You are never going to guess who I just saw," I said.

"Who?" They both asked at the same time.

"Lewis!"

"Lewis?" Noelle asked.

"Hell no! I just know you ain't talking about Loco Lewis from back home!" Brandie joked as she started laughing.

"That's exactly who I'm talking about and trust me, this isn't funny!"

"I was laughing because I seriously didn't think you were talking about him. Lewis is here... in Miami?" Brandie asked.

"YES!!"

"How did you see him?" Noelle asked.

"I was about to get in my car when I heard someone calling my name. I turned around and there he was. Y'all my nerves are so bad I'm shaking," I said.

"Are you on your way home?" Noelle asked.

"Yes, I'm too shaken up to go anywhere else."

"Okay, we'll meet you there," she said.

"Yea babe, just drive carefully. We're on our way," Brandie said.

"Thanks y'all."

I ended the call with them and breathed a sigh of relief. However, I didn't feel any kind of relief. Lewis had scared the shit out of me. Have you ever had a stalker? Have you ever had one while still in high school? Lewis had made the last few months of high school the worst time ever instead of the best time. It seemed as if everywhere I went, he was there. And he wasn't just there. He was there looking at me and watching everything I did.

He showed up at the grocery stores, the clubs, the library... just everywhere. Not to mention the fact that he called me all the time. I changed my phone number so many times I didn't even want a phone anymore. When we finally moved to Miami, I was able to relax and be myself because I no longer had to worry about Lewis showing up everywhere. Now, I no longer felt that way because Lewis was here.

I felt so violated after seeing him. I guess I had gotten too comfortable over the past couple of years. I finally made it back home and pulled into the garage. Tripp's truck was gone, so I knew he had probably gone down to the jewelry store. I was hoping that he'd be here when I got here, but I knew he had a job to do. After parking my car and closing the garage door, I made my way inside the house.

I couldn't believe Lewis was in Miami. Everything had been going perfectly for me. I knew it was too good to be true. I knew something was going to happen to fuck shit up. Why now though? Why when things were so good, and I was super happy did this have to happen?

Chapter eleven

Lewis

I hadn't seen Wynter in almost three years, but that didn't change her one bit. She was still the most beautiful girl in the world to me. I had missed her like crazy, and even though she wasn't as thrilled to see me as I was to see her, eventually, I'd have my girl back. So what if she said she was getting married in three months. She could think that if she wanted to, but I knew for a fact that it wasn't going to happen. I wasn't about to let my girl marry some nigga she met in passing. I wasn't worried about that nigga because Wynter and I had history.

I was devastated when Wynter and I broke up. I understood why she ended things with me. I mean, I had cheated on her, but damn. I thought I deserved a second chance. That was just my first offense since we had been dating. She wasn't willing to hear me out or anything. She was just adamant about ending things with me and I couldn't change her mind at all.

I remembered the day she ended things with me like it was yesterday. Would you like to know why I remembered it that well? Because I cried like a damn punk ass nigga. Wynter was literally my everything. She was a great listener and growing up in a household where I felt unappreciated, I needed that. She listened to everything and gave me some good and sound advice, which I tried to follow.

However, when it came down to her, I wasn't about to listen to her tell me that she didn't want me... that she didn't want us. That was something I wasn't willing to hear. Wynter and I belonged together. She was smart, funny, beautiful, and she cared a lot about people. I wanted us to be together, but she didn't want that.

I knew it was risky moving to Miami, but when I found out that she was out here, I had to make the move. I had every intention of getting Wynter back. We belonged together. I saw the surprised expression on her face when she realized it was me. I watched the surprise expression change the more we spoke. By the time she left, the expression had changed to frightened. She didn't have any reason to be afraid of me though. I'd never do anything to hurt Wynter. I loved her.

The only reason I was here was so she could realize how much she loved and missed me too. Then we could ride off into the sunset. What I hadn't banked on was her telling me that she was getting married. Who the hell was she marrying? Whoever it was, she hadn't known him as long as she had known me. In my eyes, she should've waited to get to know him better before accepting a marriage proposal from him. Marriage was definitely nothing that should be entered into lightly.

I was ready for marriage, and I believed that she should be married to me. We've known each other longer. I knew her likes, dislikes, pet peeves. Hell, I bet I knew more about her than her man did. I'd change her mind about marrying that nigga. She deserved more. She deserved me. I didn't come all the way to Miami to not marry that woman.

So, with that being said, I had some investigating to do. I needed to find out where she worked, where she lived, and more importantly, who the hell she was marrying. I saw that rock on her finger, so I guess the nigga had money. Shit, I had money too, so we could definitely compete for her. I loved a challenge.

As I watched her peel out of the parking lot, my first instinct was to follow her. But there was no need for that. I was way too smooth for that shit. I would just hire a private investigator to dig up all the information that I needed to find out what I wanted to know. I wasn't going to be deterred from my agenda. At the end of the day, I would get my woman back.... PERIOD!!

Chapter twelve

Noelle

The brunch this morning was awesome. That restaurant had really done their thing. The food was delicious, the atmosphere was relaxing, and the company was fantastic. I had an amazing time. Afterward, I got in my car and was headed back to the house to wait for Zach. We had a date to walk along the beach this evening. When Wynter called my phone, I thought it might be because she had forgotten to tell me something. When I heard Brandie on the line also, I wondered what was going on. I could hear the panic in Wynter's voice, so I hoped Tripp and her parents were okay.

When Wynter mentioned Lewis, I almost thought I had heard her wrong. What the hell was Lewis doing out here and how the hell did he find her? I had an eerie feeling about his presence in Miami. As I rushed over to her and Tripp's place, I called Zach to let him know that something came up.

"Hey babe," he answered.

"Hey, what are you doing?"

"Getting ready to go meet up with you. Is the luncheon over?"

"Yea, that's actually why I'm calling. Something came up and I have to go over to Wynter's place. I'm not sure how long I'll be, so I'll call you when I get back home," I said.

"Are you sure this is a Wynter emergency and not..."

"Don't say it! You have to learn to trust me Zach. I know I was wrong for lying before, but we have to put that in the past. I'm going over to Wynter's and that's the truth."

I hated when he didn't believe me, but I knew I had no one to blame for that but myself. I lied and got caught with O'Shea. I was the one who put that doubt in him. I was the one to blame for him not being able to trust me. But if we were going to continue with this relationship, he had to learn to let it go so he could trust me again. Otherwise, we weren't going to make it.

"Okay. Just call me when you get back, no matter what time it is."

"I will. I love you," I said.

"I love you too."

We ended the call and 15 minutes later, I pulled into the driveway of Tripp's huge house. This man had really done well for himself. I was proud of Wynter for giving him a chance. She could have and would have missed out on a good man if she hadn't. Brandie pulled up as I was getting out of the car. She also had a worried expression on her face.

As we walked up to the front door, I pushed the doorbell. A couple of seconds later, Wynter pulled back the huge door. She looked as if she had been crying. I immediately felt protective of my best friend. I reached out to her and she stepped into my embrace. As Brandie and I held her she cried.

After a few minutes, we walked her over to the sofa.

"Are you okay?" Brandie asked.

"No. How can I be okay when Lewis is here in Miami?"

"Damn. How the hell did he find you?" I asked.

"I don't know. He tried to make it seem like a coincidence that we ran into each other, but in my heart I know it wasn't. He's out here and he's stalking me just like he was back home!" Wynter cried.

"Have you spoken to Tripp about Lewis?" Brandie asked.

"No. Tripp doesn't know anything about him because I didn't see a reason to discuss him!"

"Well, now might be a good time to have that conversation with Tripp," Brandie said.

"Yea, I'm sure if you speak to Tripp about Lewis, he'll handle that lil maggot!" I said.

"I never wanted to discuss Lewis with Tripp..."

"You have to Wynter. There's no other way to get around it," I said.

"Yes, you have to tell Tripp about Lewis. Maybe he'll take him out and free the world of one less critter," Brandie said.

"What?! Contrary to what I thought when I first met Tripp, he isn't a thug. He's not some gangbanger who goes around shooting people and 'taking them out'! If he was, I wouldn't be with him because that's not the type of person I am!" Wynter said.

"I know that! I was just kidding!" Brandie said.

"Now isn't the time to kid around Brandie! This is my life we are talking about!"

"Look, before one of us says something we'll regret, let's take it down a notch. I'm sure Brandie didn't mean anything by what she said. But on a more serious note, you definitely need to talk to Tripp about this," I said.

"Talk to Tripp about what?" Tripp asked as he walked in. Shit, we had been going at it so much we hadn't even heard him pull into the garage.

"Hey babe," Wynter said as she rushed over to him. "I didn't hear you come in."

"Obviously. What were the three of you talking about?" he asked as he looked at Wynter. "Have you been crying? What's going on?"

Wynter turned to look at me and Brandie. Shit, she needed to tell him about Lewis so he could keep an eye on her.

"What are you ladies hiding from me?" Tripp asked.

"Babe let's sit down," Wynter said as she led him to the sofa. He sat down next to her and waited for her to say what was on her mind. She took a deep breath before she began speaking again. "Okay, when I was in high school, I used to date a guy name Lewis. I broke up with him when I found out he had cheated on me. Lewis didn't take it well."

"Didn't take it well is an understatement! The dude went cuckoo for her cocoa puffs!" Brandie said.

"What does that mean?" Tripp asked, confusion written all over his handsome face.

"It means the dude went crazy! He started following her everywhere she went, calling her nonstop... he was basically stalking her!" Brandie said.

"Okay, so some dude was stalking you in high school. What does that have to do with why you're so upset now?" Tripp asked Wynter.

"He's here... in Miami," Wynter said as she started crying again.

Tripp put his arms around her and held her close as he looked at Brandie and I for answers. "He showed up after the brunch earlier," I said.

"What?! Did he hurt you?" he asked Wynter.

She shook her head no. "No, it was just the way he spoke to me that scared me. He wanted to do lunch, but I let him know that I was engaged and had a lot to do for the wedding. The way he looked at me though... it literally sent chills down my spine," Wynter explained.

"How did he find you?" Tripp asked.

"I don't know. He made it seem like it was a coincidence that we just happened to be at the same place, but babe, it didn't feel like a coincidence. I was so scared," Wynter said.

"You don't have to worry about him. I'll handle him. Let me get his name," Tripp said as he pulled out his phone. Wynter gave his name and he pulled out his phone. As he walked out of the room, I heard him on the phone giving Lewis' name to someone.

"Humph. I knew Tripp would handle it. Shit, he may not be a gangbanger, but I bet he'll get the job done," Brandie said.

"I know he will, so you'll have nothing to worry about," I said as I wrapped an arm around Wynter's shoulder.

"I hope y'all are right."

Shit, I hope we were right too.

Two weeks later...

I had been blessed not to have heard from O'Shea the past few months. Wynter's wedding was only four weeks away and he was supposed to be one of the groomsmen. I hoped that when I saw him, it wouldn't be weird. Wynter and Tripp were having a party to celebrate their upcoming nuptials this evening and I was looking forward to that party. It had been so stressful the past couple of months seeing as how Lewis was in our area. He had been calling Wynter nonstop, so she changed her number. We didn't even know how he got her number, but Tripp was adamant about keeping Lewis away from her.

We all were meeting Wynter at their place to get our makeup done and get dressed. The party was being held at the Skydeck Rooftop which was a beautiful rooftop venue overlooking the entire city. The party was set to begin at 7:00 and the DJ was to arrive an hour ahead of that time to get the equipment set up. The event was being catered so we didn't have to worry about anything. Rebecca, the party and wedding planner had been on point since the day she was hired, so I knew the event would be great.

The guests were told to wear white considering it was an all-white party. I was excited and happy for my BFF. She deserved everything that Tripp had to offer her.

They deserved each other. As we finished putting the final touches on our hair and makeup, I admired myself in the mirror.

Wynter walked up to me and whispered, "Can I speak to you in private for a minute?"

"Sure." She had a serious expression on her face, so I wondered what the deal was. Once we had stepped out of the room, I asked, "What's going on?"

"I just wanted you to know that O'Shea would be at the party tonight," she said.

Dammit! Just when I thought I was in the clear. "Oh," was all I managed to say.

"I don't think he'll bother you though. Did you know that he was in rehab the past couple of months?"

"Rehab? Like drug rehab?" I didn't know that fool had a drug problem.

"Actually, it was a sexual addiction rehab facility..."

"A WHAT?!!" I was in total shock to hear that shit. I knew that O'Shea had problems, but I didn't know they were this bad.

"Yes. He had apparently been abusing Felicia and her friend Rhianna for months. They both agreed not to press charges if he went to the rehab center. Of course, his dad stepped in on that one because had it been up to O'Shea, he didn't think he had a problem," she said with a smirk.

"What do you mean abusing Felicia and Rhianna? Your friend Felicia?" I asked.

"Yea. That's why she rushed out of the bridal shop that day. She didn't know that we knew O'Shea, so when y'all mentioned him in conversation, she said she felt sick to her stomach."

"Why didn't she say anything to us?" I asked.

"Because you guys are strangers to her. Well, y'all have gotten to spend more time with her since then, but that day y'all had just met her. That wasn't really a conversation to have when you first meet someone," Wynter said.

"Agreed. Brandie and I suspected that she was being abused by someone, but we didn't know it was O'Shea. Talk about a small world huh?"

"Yea. Well, his dad and the girls kind of backed him into a corner to get help. If they hadn't forced him, he'd be in jail. So, I just wanted to give you a head's up that he would be there tonight. Hopefully, he'll be on his best behavior and won't cause any problems. Tripp said he's like a totally different person these days," Wynter said.

"Well, we'll just have to see huh?" I asked.

"Yep. So, let's go check on everyone else so we can get outta here. The last thing I need is to be late to my own event."

"Right, especially since black people are always late for everything."

The two of us laughed as we walked out of the room. We met with the other girls and walked out to where the party bus was waiting for us. I hope tonight would be a great night, but when O'Shea was around, you never knew.

Chapter thirteen

O'Shea

Tonight, Tripp and Wynter were having a party to celebrate their upcoming wedding. I was happy for them, and glad that I was out of the addiction center to attend. I couldn't believe I had been locked up in that facility for the past nine weeks. My dad had arranged for me to check into the facility after our last conversation. He thought that I had been going a little overboard lately and after attending group counseling and meetings at the center, I'd have to agree with him. I was totally out of line with my behavior toward women. I never should've treated Sassy that way because she was a good girl. I shouldn't have treated Noelle that way either, but the past was the past.

My therapist advised me to apologize to both women in order to close the chapter on that shit. I had apologized to Rhianna over and over again and thank God she had forgiven me for everything. I had also apologized to Felicia, but she claimed she wasn't ready to accept it yet. I didn't know what else I could do but to apologize. I definitely wasn't about to kiss her ass. I wasn't on that level anymore. At one time, I would've kissed, sucked and fucked her ass. Now, I only had eyes for one woman.

As for Noelle, I planned to apologize to her when I saw her this evening. I hope she'd be able to find it in her heart to forgive me. Shit, if I were in her shoes, I might not be able to forgive me, but I could only try.

As I stood in the mirror getting dressed, my girl came from behind me to fix my tie. "Let me get that for you," she said as she moved in front of me.

As she fixed my tie, I smiled. It was hard to believe that she and I were in the place that we were in right now. I was happy that she and I were able to get past everything that I had done to her. "There... all done," she said as she kissed me.

"Have I ever told you how much I love and appreciate you?" I asked as I held her by the waist.

She smiled and blushed. "Yes, but you can tell me again."

"I love you so much. No one has ever rocked or rode for me the way you have. I thought after I went to rehab you would've been done with me. When I wrote you that first letter, I never thought you'd respond, but you did."

"I did."

"Why? Why didn't you walk away like everybody else?" I asked.

"Because my heart wouldn't let me. I really love you Shea, like for real, for real. If you hadn't written me that first letter, I probably would've just moved on. But when you hit me up, I was excited to hear from you. I had been missing you those two weeks that you were gone before you sent me that letter. That's when I realized how real my feelings for you were," she said.

"I'm so sorry for everything I put you through. You didn't deserve any of that shit," I said.

"You've already apologized, and I've already forgiven you."

"How did I get so lucky?"

"You just happened to come across the right one," she smiled as she kissed me again. As she slipped her tongue in my mouth, she moaned.

I stopped the kiss because I knew if I didn't stop it right now, we wouldn't make it to the party on time. I didn't want to be too late. People probably didn't think I'd show up. Shit, if it wasn't for Rhianna and my dad, I probably would've been locked up in some jail cell for murder. I didn't know why I hadn't recognized that I had a problem sooner.

"Look, we need to stop this shit because if we continue this way, I'm gonna be late for the party."

"Okay. Let me go put my shoes on and refresh my lipstick and I'll be ready to go," she said.

She hurried off to finish getting ready. I checked out my reflection in the mirror and was satisfied with my appearance. My girl had bought me a white double-breasted Stacy Adams suit and some black Stacy Adams shoes to match. I chose a purple tie to complete the outfit. I looked good as fuck. I had a fresh cut and shave, so my goatee and facial hair was also on point. Rhianna walked out of the bathroom in her white lace mini dress, the top and middle were sheer lace and over her breasts and around her bottom half was white chiffon material. The dress was beautiful, and it looked great on her. I didn't want Wynter to think that my girl was trying to upstage her since she was the bride.

When she was ready, I grabbed the keys and we headed out the door. The ride to the venue took only 20 minutes. I was anxious to see how the rooftop venue looked since I had never been there. After I parked and locked the car, Rhianna and I walked inside hand in hand.

"Are you nervous?" she asked.

"Not really. Are you?"

"A little. This is the first time we're attending an event as a couple."

"The first, but not the last."

She held my hand tighter as we walked toward the elevator. As we rode in the elevator in silence with a few other people in white, I thought about how right my dad was to insist I get help. Who knows where I would've been right now if he hadn't helped me? The elevator dinged to the top floor and we exited the elevator. The party was in full swing as we made our way through the entourage of people.

I saw Tripp and Travis and a couple of other groomsmen chopping it up, so I headed over there to where they stood. I still held on to Rhianna's hand.

"Do you wanna go holla at the girls?" I asked.

"Yea, I do. However, I'd like to meet your friends first if that's alright. I've heard a lot about Tripp from the girls, so I'm kind of anxious to meet him," she said.

I had no problem with that. Had it been before rehab, I would've knocked her head from side to side. But this was a new and better version of myself, so I wasn't the least bit jealous that she wanted to meet my best friend. As a matter of fact, I wanted her to meet Tripp. He and I had been through a lot together and I owed him a whole lot.

We walked up to the fellas and they greeted me with brotherly hugs. I even hugged Travis. He and I had also been through a lot together. I wanted him to know that even though he was now with Tamika, I didn't hold any ill feelings toward him. If that was who he wanted, more power to him.

"Wassup y'all?" I asked. "I'd like to introduce y'all to my girl Rhianna. Rhianna, this is Tripp the groom and my best friend, Travis, Don, Chris, and Thomas. Sorry man, I can't recall your name." I was sure if I thought hard enough, I'd remember Noelle's friend's name, but I didn't feel the need to dig that deep.

"It's Zach. Nice to meet you Rhianna," he said.

The rest of the men greeted Rhianna and then she turned and gave me a kiss before walking off to join Felicia and the girls. I noticed Noelle looking good as hell. I couldn't believe how good she looked. She had slimmed down a whole lot. She wore a beautiful white dress with a plunging neckline and her big boobs sitting high on her chest. I decided to excuse myself and go over there to speak to her. Now was as good a time as any to tell her how sorry I was.

"Excuse me ladies. Noelle, may I speak to you for a minute?"

"Me?" Noelle asked as she pointed to herself.

"Yea. If that's okay." I saw the mouths on the other women drop, almost as if I was an alien speaking to them.

"Okay."

We walked a short distance away from everyone. "You look amazing. How've you been?" I asked.

"I've been really good. I'm happier than I've ever been," she said.

I'd be lying if I said that didn't make me feel some kind of way. How could she be happier than she had ever been? Wasn't she happy with me? Who was I kidding? Of course, shit with me wasn't as good as they were for her now. I was the worst nigga in the world for her and I treated her like shit.

"That's good. I'm really happy for you," I said with a smile.

"Thank you. How've you been?"

"I've been great! That's kind of what I wanted to talk to you about. I just wanted to apologize to you for everything I put you through," I said.

"Wow! This is a shock."

"I know. I'm sorry it took me this long to admit that I was wrong... on so many levels. I shouldn't have done any of that shit to you. You're a good woman Noelle and you deserve to be as happy as you are. I'm sorry I couldn't be the one to make you this happy," I said.

Whether she believed me or not, I really meant what I said. Even if Noelle wasn't happy with me, I was glad she had found someone to make her smile. She reached up and put her hand to my forehead. I smiled and asked, "What are you doing?"

"Checking to see if you're running a fever." We both burst into laughter.

"Nah, no fever. I'm just doing something I should've done a long time ago. I hope that you can find it in your heart to forgive me."

"I forgave you a long time ago O'Shea."

"Wow! Really?"

"Yes really. Forgiveness isn't for the person who needs it. It's really for the person who grants it. If I can't forgive you, I'd never be able to move on and be happy," she said.

"I hadn't thought about that, but I guess you're right. But look, I wish you and what's his name? Zach?" She nodded and glanced over to where he was. "I wish y'all the best of luck."

"Thanks, I appreciate that. I saw you come in with Rhianna. Are you guys back together?"

"Oh, you knew about her?"

"Yea, well, Felicia is one of Wynter's bridesmaids, so we met Rhianna through her."

"Yea, we trying to make something happen."

"That's good. She seems like a nice person," Noelle said.

"Yea, she is. She's had my back the way you used to, even when I didn't deserve it."

"Well, she's definitely a keeper." We laughed for a brief moment. It felt really good to laugh with Noelle. It made me feel as if she truly forgave me.

"Well, I'ma let you get back to your girls. Have a good night," I said.

"Yea, you too."

I turned and walked over to Rhianna. I felt like dancing with my girl, so I approached her and whispered in her ear, "Can you dance with me?"

"Oh yes," she said with a smile.

She took my hand and we headed to the dance floor. As I sang Jaheim's, *You Can Have Anything* in her ear, I could second Noelle's emotion. This was the happiest I had ever been also. Thinking back to where I was a few months ago seemed like years, but I knew that I wasn't out of the woods yet. I still had to see my therapist once or twice a week and I was on medication to control my temperament. Yea, who would've thought?

But if I wanted to continue acting right, those were the conditions I had to follow. I had no problem obeying the rules though. As long as I got to be just as happy as my friends were, I was good. I watched Tamika as she roamed around the room with a big belly. I was glad that she was pregnant with Travis' seed. It was better than her being pregnant with my kid. I mean, you can't turn a ho' into a housewife, but Travis could try.

Everybody deserved to be loved by someone, right? As I held Rhianna closer, I continued to serenade her as she giggled in my ear. I watched as Noelle and Zach took to the dance floor. After a few minutes, Tripp and Wynter, along with Brandie and Nelson joined us on the dance floor. Everyone seemed to be having a great time.

After a few minutes, it was time for the food to be served. We all took our seats as the servers began to distribute our plates. There were three choices... filet mignon, stuffed flounder, and baked chicken. There were also different sides to choose from... green beans, mashed potatoes, asparagus, vegetable medley and a few others. When we arrived, we were given our menus and told to place our orders because dinner was going to be served at eight o'clock on the dot. That was pretty cool. It was really beautiful up here with the city's skyline all lit up.

There were white sofas and clear glass coffee tables spread about, but we were seated at long tables surrounded by white chairs. I had never seen a place so beautiful. Tripp and Wynter sure knew how to scout out venues, for sure.

As we ate, Rhianna and I spoke about how pretty everything was. She was in awe of the view from the rooftop, so was I. A couple of times during dinner, I caught Noelle looking at me. I smiled and so did she. I was trying to read her expressions, but I couldn't. After dinner, I decided to make a toast to the happy couple.

As I cleared my throat, I stood up and grabbed my glass. "Will everyone grab their glasses please?" Everyone picked their glasses up. "I'd just like to give a special congratulations to my brother, Tripp and his bride, Wynter. Tripp, you and I have been through a lot over the years, bro. You stuck by me through all my foolishness and made sure that I was straight when I needed you the most. You looked out for me at times when no one else would. I know that I don't always say it, but I love and appreciate you so much bro. Wynter, I don't know you that well, but what I do know is that you found a real one in Tripp. I can tell that the two of you love each other very much and I wish you nothing but the best. To the happy couple, I salute you." Everyone lifted their glasses, took a sip, then set them down on the table as I walked over to hug my brother and his bride to be, the room erupted in applause.

"I love you man. I mean that," I whispered to Tripp as we hugged. I'd be lying if I said I wasn't teary eyed, but I'm a real dude so I wasn't about to let anybody see that shit.

"I love you too man. I'm glad you could be here," Tripp said.

"There's no place I'd rather be." And that was the truth.

I reached in for a hug from Wynter and she hugged me with tears in her eyes. "That was so beautiful. Thank you," she whispered.

"You're welcome. Thanks for letting me be a part of your special day," I said.

"We're glad you could be here."

We released each other and I walked back to my seat. The dinner plates were removed from the table and replaced with dessert, a triple layer of carrot cake. I was glad it wasn't chocolate considering everyone was dressed in white. I sat down next to Rhianna.

"That was a beautiful speech babe," she whispered as she leaned in for a kiss.

I was more than happy to plant one on her. Rhianna had been through it all with me and she still loved me. I knew that she was the one for me, and I planned to make it official. My dad had given me my mom's engagement ring and Tripp had upgraded it for me. I planned to ask Rhianna to marry me, but not here. This was Tripp's night and the last thing I wanted to do was take the spotlight off of him and his lady.

My phone beeped with a text message, so I pulled it from my pocket. It was a text from Tripp...

Tripp: What are you waiting for? Ask her

Me: I didn't wanna do that now. It's your night
Tripp: Do it!

I looked over at him and he winked and raised his glass. I took a deep breath and stood up. I reached my hand out to Rhianna and she stared at me confusingly. "What are you up to?" she asked with a smile.

"Do you trust me?"

"With my life," she said as she slipped her hand in mine.

She stood up and I stared into her eyes. "Babe, I've put you through so much shit over the past few months. So much, that the average woman would've walked out by now, but not you. You stuck by me and held me down through it all. Your love for me never wavered and grew stronger. I just want you to know that I love you and if you let me, I'll love you for the rest of our lives," I said as I got down on one knee.

"Oh my God! What are you doing?" she asked as tears sprang to her eyes.

"Rhianna, I love you. You've proven to me that you're the only woman in the world for me. So, I just wanna know if you'll marry me. Rhianna Thomas will you be my wife?" I asked.

I opened the box and showed her the sparkling two carat diamond ring. Tripp had done an awesome job upgrading the diamond, but it was set in the same white gold band my mom wore.

"Oh my God! YES!" I stood up and kissed her hard and full on the mouth. As we embraced, I caught Noelle's eyes on me again. Her eyes were sparkling like she had tears in them. I wondered why she was crying, but that wasn't my concern. The only woman I was worried about was my fiancée.

I pulled back from her and placed the ring on her finger. She gazed at it and hugged me again. "I can't believe you did this!"

"I love you," I said.

"I love you too baby."

People gathered around us to congratulate us. I felt really good about the decision I had made. Rhianna deserved the best and I'd make sure to give that to her.

Chapter fourteen

Noelle

When Wynter pulled me to the side to tell me that O'Shea would be at her dinner party tonight, I was shocked. I hadn't seen or heard from him in almost three months. I had wondered what was going on with him and if he was okay, but never checked on him. He wasn't my concern anymore, so anything he had going on was his business, not mine. I didn't care if he showed up at the dinner or not. If he tried to speak to me, I was going to remain cordial and keep it moving.

However, when I laid eyes on him, my heart skipped the same beat it did when we first met. He looked amazing in his white suit. He had a fresh haircut, his eyes looked brighter, and he had a style about him that exuded confidence. It was like when he walked in the room, his presence demanded attention. I couldn't help but stare at him.

I also couldn't help but notice he was with Rhianna. As I watched the two of them, I felt a tinge of jealousy course through my body. I didn't even know the two of them were still together. I thought she would've walked away once he had been admitted into that rehab facility, but apparently not. When I saw him approaching us, I almost shitted on myself. I didn't know why my body and heart were acting this way over a man who had used and abused me. I had a great man now, so why was I so excited that O'Shea wanted to speak to me in private.

The conversation between us was better than I could've expected. We laughed, he apologized, and everything was all good. I expected him to ask about me and my relationship with Zach, but he didn't. He mentioned me looking happy, which I was, but that was it.

As he spoke, I inhaled his cologne. He smelled so fucking good. I was glad he hadn't tried to hug me because if he had, I knew I would've melted in his arms. After talking for a few minutes, I walked away feeling more confused than ever. I loved Zach, right? Of course, I loved Zach. But if I truly loved Zach, why was I feeling this way about O'Shea?

As we sat down to eat dinner, I found myself gazing at him several times. Zach was making conversation, but I wasn't really hearing him. My eyes were stuck on O'Shea and the conversation he was having with Rhianna. The exchange between the two of them reminded me of Tripp and Wynter. Was he really in love with that stripper? How could he be in love with a woman who shed her clothes on a stage for men to see?

When our dinner was over, I watched as O'Shea stood up and made a toast to Wynter and Tripp. I'd be lying if I said his toast wasn't touching. Tears sprung to my eyes as I listened to his heartfelt words which held so much emotion. I could tell that he meant every single word that came out of his mouth. O'Shea seemed to be a changed man, and for some reason, I was loving it.

As I wiped a tear from my eye, Zach leaned in. "Are you okay?"

"Yea, I'm fine."

"You sure?"

"Don't I look fine Zach? I mean, it was a touching speech," I said.

As I continued to watch O'Shea, I noticed him checking and texting on his phone while looking at Tripp. I guess they were discussing something they didn't want anyone else to know about. It made me wonder what the hell the two of them had planned? When O'Shea stood up and took that girl's hand, I almost died. Whatever he was about to do, I prayed it wasn't a proposal. That dude wasn't ready to get married... and he certainly wasn't ready to marry no stripper. I really wished men would stop and think things through before making split-second decisions.

Sure enough, he got down on one knee and asked the ho' to marry him. I was floored. How could he ask her to marry him? What the hell had they been through together that would make him think she was the one? She said yes! Why would she marry him when he had whooped her ass? That was some straight bullshit!

I didn't even notice I had tears in my eyes until one fell on my hand. I had to excuse myself because this shit was ridiculous. I left from the table and rushed to the restroom. I entered a stall and grabbed some tissue to dab at my eyes before my fucking eyelashes came off and my makeup start running.

KNOCK! KNOCK! KNOCK!

"This one is occupied!" I said.

"Duh! I know it is. Zach asked me to check on you. Are you alright?" Brandie asked.

"I'm fine Brandie. Go back and join the others!"

"Why does it sound like you crying girl? Noelle what's going on with you?"

"Nothing. Can you just leave me alone?" I asked hoping that she would leave the restroom.

"No, I cannot! Your man is wondering where you are and if you're okay. Do you want me to go out there and tell him that you in here crying over O'Shea?"

I opened the door and locked eyes with her. "You better not!"

"Seriously though, what's wrong with you? Because I know you ain't really in here crying over O'Shea's sorry ass. I was just clowning to get you to come out the restroom," Brandie said. I guess my hesitation to respond spoke volumes. "Are you serious?"

"What?"

"You're really crying over that nigga?"

"No!" I lied.

"Then what? What could have you in here crying when you're supposed to be out there with Zach?"

"I don't know. It doesn't really matter how I'm feeling right now, this isn't the time or place to talk about it. So, can we just drop it until later?" I asked.

"Yea, you best believe we'll be discussing it later," she said.

I made my way to the sink and mirror to inspect my makeup. I dabbed at my eyes once more before we left the restroom. Once I made it back to the table, Zach immediately stood up. He pulled out my chair and as I sat down, he asked, "Are you okay?"

"I told you I'm fine. You don't have to keep asking me that," I said with a smile.

I didn't want him to get suspicious about how I was acting. I didn't want to seem rude to him either. Zach was a great guy and I did love him... at least I thought I did. Now, my feelings were going haywire. I didn't know how I felt right now.

Tripp clinked his glass to get everyone's attention. "I'd like to propose a toast to the woman of my dreams, my queen and bride to be. I never knew that love could feel this way. You brighten all my days, even when they're a bit cloudy. You give me strength, even when I'm feeling weak. You give me love, even when sometimes I don't think I deserve it. You have made me a better person. I thank God every day that you gave me a chance and decided to get to know me. I love you so much and I can't wait to make you my wife," he said with a huge smile. Wynter's eyes were filled with tears as she smiled and gazed into his eyes lovingly. "I need you all to raise your glasses please and salute my beautiful future wife. I love you Wynter!"

"I love you too," she said as they shared a sweet kiss.

I loved their relationship. They just meshed and loved each other. You could just look at them and could tell that they were in love. I had wanted that for me and Zach. I wanted us to have that kind of love, and I thought we had it... until tonight. After seeing O'Shea and being around him, now I wasn't so sure. I didn't know what I wanted anymore.

Zach asked me to dance, but I declined. I just didn't feel like dancing with him. As I watched O'Shea tear the floor up with that stripper, I felt some kind of way. Why wasn't he feeling as deflated as I was? Why didn't he feel my pain?

"Are you ready to go?" Zach asked.

"You can go. I'm gonna catch a ride home with Brandie."

"I thought you were coming over to my house for the night?"

"I don't feel like it anymore, but I'll give you a call tomorrow," I said.

"Wow!"

"Wow what?"

"Everything was fine before that nigga walked in the room. Now, it's like you stuck on stupid for that nigga all over again," he said.

"Oh, so now I'm stupid?" I asked feeling myself growing angry.

"I sat here next to you all night and watched you having googly eyes for that nigga. I watched you shed tears when he asked his lady to marry him. I saw how you ran out of here upset when she said yes. And now, now you're telling me you don't want to leave with me. I get it Noelle!" he said with tears in his eyes. "I thought you would appreciate a man who could love you like you deserved to be loved. I thought you wanted a man who could treat you like the queen you are. But you don't!

You're still in love with the same nigga that walked all over you and treated you like shit!"

He stood up and walked away from the table, leaving me sitting there feeling like shit. I never meant to hurt Zach. I don't even know why I'm behaving this way. I glanced over at the dance floor and O'Shea was slow dancing with Rhianna while whispering in her ear. I could see her giggling as her diamond on her left hand sparkled under the night sky. They looked really happy, but sometimes looks could be deceiving. Just because one person looked happy, that didn't necessarily mean they were.

When I saw the girl pry herself from his arms and walk inside, I figured she was going to the restroom. I made my way to where O'Shea stood as he waited for her to return. As the smooth sounds of Luther Vandross' Always and Forever flowed through the speakers, I snuck up on O'Shea.

"Can I have this dance?" I asked.

"Uh, I don't know if that would be a good idea," he said as he looked around.

"C'mon! What's one dance between friends? Is your girl that jealous?" I teased.

"Nah, she straight. She know she ain't got shit to worry about."

Damn. That shit stung!

"So, you gonna dance with me?"

"Yea, sure."

He followed me to the dance floor and took me into his arms. I felt as if I was melting from his touch. Oh my God! It felt so good to be in his arms.

"Where's your man?" he asked.

"He went home," I said.

"Really? So, he just left you here by yourself?"

"I wanted to be left alone. I have a lot on my mind..."

"Yea, like what?"

"It's not important," I said.

"So, tell me this."

"What?"

"Why are you here dancing with me instead of home with your man?" O'Shea asked.

"I don't really have an answer for you right now."

"Just be honest."

"I don't think you're ready for me to be honest," I said.

"Probably not."

"I thought so."

"Look Noelle, I just want you to know how happy I am for you. I'm glad you found someone to make you happy, especially since I didn't do a good job at that," he said.

"It wasn't all your fault," I said. Shit, I didn't even know where that statement came from. I had blamed everything on O'Shea this whole time. Why was I trying to take some of that blame off of him now?

"What?" Shit, he was probably just as surprised to hear me say that as I was to say it.

"Excuse me," came the female voice from behind me. I rolled my eyes and turned to look at her. "May I have my fiancé back please?"

"Yea, sure. It was good to see you again O'Shea. Congrats again on your engagement," I said as I walked off.

My mind was all over the damn place. I didn't know where these feelings for O'Shea were coming from. Maybe it was the champagne that was fucking with me. As I stood to the side watching him and his fiancée dance happily, my stomach began to churn. How could he be happy with a woman who had showed her cookies to all kinds of strange men? If I were in his shoes, I wouldn't want to marry that kind of woman.

I decided to go home. Staying here was making me miserable. I went over to Tripp and Wynter to let them know that I was leaving.

"Hey guys, your party was fantastic! I had a great time, but I'm gonna cut out now."

"Oh okay. Where's Zach?" Wynter asked as she looked around.

"He left a while ago."

"He left you here by yourself?" Tripp asked.

"That doesn't sound like him," Wynter chimed in.

"Yea, well, I insisted."

Wynter raised an eyebrow at me. "Babe, I'm gonna walk her out," she said.

"Alone? Aw hell nah!"

"It'll be fine. I'll get Brandie to come with us," Wynter said.

"Please be careful," Tripp said as he kissed Wynter.

"We will."

We walked away from him and motioned for Brandie to join us.

"What's up?" Brandie asked.

"We're walking Noelle out."

"You're leaving already?" Brandie asked.

"Yes, I'm suddenly not feeling so well," I lied.

"Humph," Brandie huffed as we got into the elevator car.

"What's that supposed to mean?" I asked.

"We both know that the reason you're leaving is because you're upset about O'Shea proposing to that woman!" Brandie blurted out.

Wynter gasped and turned to look at me. "Say it ain't so Noelle! After everything that he put you through, please tell me that ain't the case," she said.

"It's not!"

"It is too! I caught her crying like a baby in the restroom right after he proposed!" Brandie said. I glared at her wishing I had the ability to keep her mouth shut.

"Noelle, just because he looks different and like he has his shit together, that don't mean he's changed. Zach is a good dude, and he loves you," Wynter said.

"I know that!" I said as I poked my lip out. "I don't know what's wrong with me."

"I'll tell you what's wrong with you! You need somebody to slap some sense into you, and I could do it if you want me to!" Brandie said.

"Oh please, do it!" I said.

"I'm just saying. You finally got rid of that creep... move on. As you can see, he ain't been thinking bout you at all!"

That was really mean of her to say, but she was right. If O'Shea had been thinking about me, he never would've asked that ho' to marry him. Ugh! Now I felt worse than ever. I really needed to get outta here. I just wanted to be alone!

Chapter fifteen

Rhianna

People probably thought I was crazy for accepting a marriage proposal from O'Shea, especially after everything he had put me through. But the truth of the matter was that I was in love with him. I couldn't understand how I could feel the way that I did about him. I was just as surprised as O'Shea was that I still loved him. We had been through a whole lot the past few months. I had definitely been through more than any woman should ever have to endure. When O'Shea's dad had contacted me about him checking into rehab, I almost laughed. But at the same time, how could I?

O'Shea had serious problems at the time. He had a problem with sex and controlling women. So, once I thought about what his father said, I knew that O'Shea going to rehab would be the best thing for him. I thanked him for the information, and we ended the call. Imagine my surprise when I checked the mail one day and found a letter from O'Shea. I was shocked that he had written me, but I was happy at the same time.

The letter he wrote to me was sweet and kind. It was more than I could've hoped for. It really touched my heart when I read it. It went something like this...

Hey Sassy, I mean Rhianna. I hope everything has been going well for you and that this letter finds you in the best health. I know you're probably surprised to hear from me huh? I was sitting in here thinking about you. I miss you girl. I know I ain't been in here that long, but the whole time I've been in here all I can think about is you. You've been on my mind since day one. I've been speaking to a therapist and shit. He's been helping me realize what a troubled soul I am and how wrong I've been toward you. I just want to apologize to you. I know you might not accept it right now, and that's okay. My therapist said that it may take you some time, but I'm willing to wait on you babe. I came to realize how much I really love you. I never should've put you through all that shit. I am learning a lot about myself in here and it ain't all good shit either. I care a lot about you Rhianna. I love you. I'm gonna be here for at least a few more weeks, so I hope to hear back from you. If you ain't ready to write me back though, I understand. Just know that however you wanna proceed, I'll be here. Love O'Shea

I must have read that same letter like four or five times. I couldn't believe he called me by government name. He always referred to me as Sassy since the day we met, but today, he called me Rhianna. To some people, that may not have been a big deal. To me, it was everything. The fact that he even remembered my name meant the world to me. I held the letter against my chest as tears streamed from my eyes. He called me Rhianna. He said he loved me. He told me that he was sorry. All the things I ever wanted from him, he did it in that one letter.

As my heart pounded against the letter, I couldn't help but smile. I had missed O'Shea. Not the way he treated me, but his presence. I guess I missed his dick inside me the most. I mean, we didn't always have bad times. Sometimes, things between us were really good. I took the letter with me to my room, shut the door and did some soul searching. The reason I locked myself in my room was because if Felicia came home, I didn't want her to feel like she had any say so in how I ran my life or the decisions I chose to make.

After taking a couple of days to think about it, I decided to write him back. It was a decision I had thought long and hard about. My first letter went like this...

Hey Shea, to say that I was surprised to hear from you is an understatement. But while I was surprised, I was happy. I had been thinking about you also but didn't know where you were. I'm glad you wrote first though because it made me feel special. Thank you for apologizing and for calling me by my real name. That meant a lot to me. How are you doing over there? From what you've told me, therapy seems to be working for you. I'm glad. I guess your dad coming to visit wasn't a bad thing after all, huh? Look, you're right, the two of us have been through a lot... a whole lot. The fact that you're still able to tell me that you love me after everything we've been through... well, let's just say you made me cry. I just want you to know that I appreciate the apology and that all is forgiven. I'm glad that your therapist is helping you right your wrongs. I'm glad that he has helped you see where you were wrong. I want you to know that you can write to me anytime. If you write, I promise to write you back. If you decide to call me, my new number is 786-225-9738. It would be nice to hear your voice. Oh, by the way, I love you too. I never stopped loving you. I hope to hear from you soon. Rhianna.

I sent the letter to him and the same night he received it, he called me. The two of us spoke to each other every day after that first call and we wrote at least once a week. That was two months ago. When O'Shea was released, I picked him up from the facility. He would've stayed longer, but Tripp and Wynter had that dinner the following night. Considering he was a best man in their wedding, he chose to leave early.

I was happy because I had missed him and knowing that we were going to be together made his homecoming even more special. The dinner was an all-white event, so I went shopping the day before to get him a suit I knew he would love. I picked him up and immediately jumped out of the car and into his open arms. I wrapped my legs around his waist as he held and kissed me.

"You better stop before we have to get it in right here," he joked as he placed me on the ground.

"I'm so happy to finally feel you again," I said.

"Well, let's go to my place so you can feel all of me."

We happily got in the car and headed home. As soon as we walked through the door, it was on. I had missed this man and his sex had always been on point, even though he liked it rough. He practically tore my clothes off of me and devoured my neck in sensual kisses. Oh shit! That was something new and different and I liked it. Hell, I liked it a lot!!

O'Shea had me so wet I could feel my cream soaking my panties. When he reached for the thin material, I wasn't surprised when he ripped it off of my ass. As I stood before him butt ass naked, he licked his sexy lips. I smiled as he kissed me hungrily. I moaned as he gripped my ass cheeks in both hands. When he slid down to the floor, I gasped as I stood anticipating what was to come next. He lightly rubbed his hand against the top of my kitty. I purred with pleasure.

He lifted one of my legs onto his shoulder as I held onto the wall. He slid his tongue inside my silky wet folds causing my body to shudder. It felt heavenly as my clitoris vibrated against his top lip.

"Oh my God!" I cried out as my body shook from an intense and much needed orgasm. He continued to suck all my juices until there weren't any left.

He placed my leg on the floor and kissed me from my belly to my lips. I opened my mouth to receive his tongue and marveled at this new sensation that was taking over me. I reached for his shirt and pulled it over his head, tossing it to the floor. Then I reached for his pants and dropped them to the floor. I stroked his hardened shaft through his boxers as he moaned against my lips. I kissed his neck, his chest and dropped down to my knees, pulling his boxers off in the process. As he stepped out of his pants and boxers, I smiled as his dick came alive from being freed.

I licked the length of it, making sure to run my tongue along his balls in a circular motion. He moaned as I wrapped my lips around the mushroom head of his dick, applying gentle pressure. Then I took it all in my mouth and sucked it like my life depended on it. As he moaned, I continued to show him how much I had missed him. After a couple of minutes, he lifted me up and guided me to the bed.

As I laid on the bed, he climbed on top of me. While gazing deep into my eyes, he whispered huskily, "I'm gonna do something to you that I ain't never done to another female before."

"What's that?" I purred.

"I'm gonna make love to you," he said as he inserted his shaft inside me.

"Mmmm!" I crooned as he slowly rotated his hips while kissing me softly. I wasn't sure where this was coming from, but I was happy that I was here for it.

From that afternoon until well into the night, O'Shea and I discovered things about each other that we never knew before. Not only did he make me feel brand new, but he also paid attention to my wants and catered to my needs. But no matter how well he and I were getting along or how different this new relationship felt, I never expected him to get down on one knee and propose to me. When he asked me if I trusted him, I never thought he was asking because he wanted to ask me to marry him.

As he knelt before me, tears sprang to my eyes. After I said yes and we embraced, I noticed Noelle brushing away her own tears out of the corner of my eyes. What the heck was she crying for? Why was she so upset? I mean, surely, she didn't think that O'Shea was going to sit around waiting for her. She had her own man in her life. Maybe I was reading too much into why she was crying. It may not have anything to do with O'Shea's proposal. She might be crying because her own relationship isn't as solid as ours.

When her man left the party later and she stayed behind, I knew that had to be the case. She was feeling some kind of way about O'Shea asking me to marry him because her relationship was falling apart. I felt bad for her because she deserved to be happy too. The way I was feeling right now with this beautiful ring on my finger and sitting next to the man I loved, I just wanted everyone to be this happy. I wanted the whole world to experience the type of joy that my man and I were feeling.

"You hear that?" O'Shea asked as he leaned close to my ear.

"Hear what?"

"You don't hear that Babyface song?"

I opened my ears to the song and tried to calm the thumping of my heart. Sure enough, the DJ was playing Babyface's, *Soon As I Get Home*. A slow smile crept across my face as I nodded my head. "That's my jam," I said.

"Come tear the floor up with me," he said as he stood up and reached for my hand.

"You serious?"

"Hell yea!" I took his hand and allowed him to lead me to the middle of the dance floor. As he wrapped my arms around his neck and his around my waist, we began to slow dance to the song.

I absolutely loved the way his arms felt around me. After a couple of songs, I needed to use the restroom. The champagne was rushing to escape. "I need to go to the restroom. Behave yourself while I'm gone."

"Aye, I'm an engaged man now baby! You ain't got shit to worry about," he said as he kissed me.

For once, I believed him. I sashayed to the door and made my way to the restroom. The line was kind of long, almost as if all the women had to pee at once. I didn't sweat it though because I knew my man would be waiting for me when I got back. It took me about 10 minutes to return to him and when I did, I almost shitted on myself. He was still on the dance floor, but this time he was dancing with Noelle.

I took a deep breath and calmed my nerves. As I watched the exchange between the two of them, it seemed as if my man was just having conversation. On the other hand, Noelle looked like she was in love or something. She stared at him all dreamy eyed and shit. I didn't want to cause a scene or anything. After all, I was the one wearing the engagement ring. So, whatever thoughts she had about her and my man were just in her head.

I walked up to them and patted her lightly on the shoulder. "Excuse me, may I have my fiancé back please?"

She stepped back with a tight smile across her lips. "Yea, sure. It was good to see you again O'Shea. Congrats again on your engagement." With that, she walked off like she had fire in her panties.

I looked up at O'Shea as he took me in his arms. "What was that about?" I asked.

"Nothing for you to be concerned about. She just wanted to congratulate us, that's all."

"I don't know babe. There's something about her demeanor that seems a bit off. I think she might still be in love with you."

"Girl no! She done moved on and she's happy with her man!" he said. "We just got engaged and I'm happier than I've ever been. Let's not allow those old insecurities to rear their ugly heads and manifest again."

"Oh, I'm far from insecure. I just want her to keep her paws off my man."

"So, you're jealous?"

"No, I'm not. I just know how women can be. Even though you don't believe me, I'm telling you that she's up to something," I said.

"Well, whatever she's up to if she was up to anything, she already knows how much I love you," he said as he kissed me.

For the next couple of hours, we danced the night away putting all thoughts of Noelle to rest. I wasn't going to forget about her completely because I worked with a lot of women in my business. I knew a woman with an agenda when I saw one. But that bitch would want to stay in her lane. I had worked hard to get this man, so I wasn't about to let him go for some bitch who threw him away.

Chapter sixteen

Brandie

I couldn't believe how Noelle was acting when it came to O'Shea. She had been made a fool of by that man I don't know how many times. How could she be weeping and whining over his ass like he was such a dream catch? She actually let her man go home while she stayed behind to share a dance with O'Shea. What the fuck did she hope to accomplish from doing that? Did she think he was going to break up with his fiancée for her stupid ass? No man wants a weak woman and she was at her weakest point right now.

As Wynter and I rode down the elevator with her, it took everything in me not to slap the shit out of her. How could she treat Zach that way when he had been so good to her? What was she thinking? Hell, maybe she wasn't thinking. Maybe she was too drunk to think straight. But shit, she didn't seem drunk to me. Fuck, maybe I was drunk!

The elevator dinged to the first floor and we walked her to the door. She looked at her phone and said, "My Uber is here. I'll talk to you guys tomorrow."

She reached out to hug Wynter. "Get home safe."

"I will."

She reached out to hug me. "You better call Zach and apologize."

"Apologize for what?" she asked.

"For treating him like shit tonight... that's what! You were wrong Noelle!" I said. "I mean, how would you like if he treated you the way you did him? The way O'Shea used to treat you?"

I could see the expression change on her face, but I needed to ask that question. She needed to know that just because O'Shea seemed to be a changed man, that didn't necessarily mean that he was one. He could be the same asshole that used her for her money and abused her like a second rate ho'!

"How I handle my business with Zach is my business! While I appreciate the advice, trust me, it isn't needed. I know what I'm doing."

"Do you? Do you really? Because what I see is that you're going to lose a good man doing some stupid shit!" I said.

"When I need your advice Brandie, I'll ask for it. Until then, mind your business!" Noelle said with a grimace. "Thank you ladies for walking me down. Enjoy the rest of your evening." She plastered a fake smile on her face and walked toward the Uber that was waiting for her.

"Ugh! She is pissing me off!" I grunted.

"I know, but she's right about one thing... it's her business. We can offer advice, but it seems as if it's falling on deaf ears. I don't know about you, but I have too much going on to be worried about Noelle's love life. My wedding is in three weeks!" Wynter said.

"I know. Speaking of wedding, let's get back inside before Tripp comes looking for you," I said. We turned to head back inside when I heard Wynter yelp. "Girl, what the hell..."

My words fell off as I watched my best friend being dragged into a car by Lewis. She wasn't screaming or anything, but she had tears in her eyes. As I ran over to the car, Lewis flashed a gun in my face. "If you don't want to die right here and right now, you will get your ass back!" The scowl on his face let me know that he meant business. I slowly backed away as I kept my eyes on the gun.

He slid behind the steering wheel and took off. I began screaming for someone to help me. People began to gather around me asking what was wrong. "MY BEST FRIEND HAS BEEN KIDNAPPED BY A PSYCHO!! CALL 911 PLEASE!" I screamed.

I reached for my phone in my pocket and called Tripp. "Yo, where y'all at?"

"TRIPP!!"

"What happened?" he asked, hearing the panic in my voice.

"HE TOOK HER!!" I cried.

"WHAT?!"

"LEWIS TOOK WYNTER!!"

"GOTDAMMIT!! I KNEW I SHOULDN'T HAVE LET Y'ALL GO DOWN THERE ALONE!! WHERE ARE YOU?!" he asked.

"OUTSIDE WAITING FOR THE POLICE!" I cried. My heart was so hurt. How did this shit happen? How was Lewis able to sneak up on us without us knowing he was there? I knew how... we weren't paying attention to our surroundings. That fool had a gun. Who would give him a gun when he was clearly cuckoo?

The police arrived at the same time Tripp had made his way downstairs, followed by practically everyone else who was on the rooftop. The officers walked over to us and asked what happened. I explained to them that Lewis had kidnapped Wynter by gunpoint. They wanted a description of Lewis, the clothes he was wearing and the car he was driving. After giving the police all the necessary information they needed to find Lewis' ass, I was drained. I collapsed in Nelson's arms crying. Tripp was really flying off the handle and I couldn't say that I blamed him.

Who knew what Lewis was capable of at this point? He definitely looked off his rocker. I prayed that Wynter would be alright until they found her.

"Lord please keep my BFF safe. She's really a good and kind person and doesn't deserve anything bad to happen to her. Please save her from that lunatic. In Jesus name, I pray," I said.

Chapter seventeen

Lewis

When I found out that Wynter was getting married, I knew shit was going to go left for someone. There was no way I was going to allow my woman to marry that nigga. I didn't give a fuck who he was. Wynter belonged to me and that was all there was to it. I found out she was having a gathering at some rooftop bar. I did a little snooping and found out exactly which one. I didn't have an invitation, so I couldn't get inside. I was a little pissed about that, but what could I do about it?

Instead of throwing a fit to get inside, I just waited patiently for her to exit. If she exited with that nigga, I'd just kill his ass and take my woman. Shit, I wasn't afraid to point and shoot. I was willing to do anything to get Wynter back. I sat down in the parking lot across the street listening to music while I waited.

It took about two hours before she finally brought her ass outside the building. I saw her and her two friends having some heated discussion, so I moved my car behind the taxi cab and Uber driver. After Noelle got in the car and it drove off, I slipped out of the car and rushed over quietly as they were walking back inside of the building. I wrapped my arm around her waist with the gun out of sight but making sure that she knew it was there.

She yelped when I grabbed her which alerted Brandie's fat ass that I was there.

"You need to move quietly with me to my car or I will kill you," I threatened.

By the time Brandie realized what was going on, I had shoved Wynter in the car. She rushed up and I quickly pointed the gun at her, threatening to blow her fucking head off. I would've done it too if she hadn't backed off. I didn't give a fuck about her ass, only Wynter.

Once we had taken off, Wynter looked at me with tears in her eyes. She really looked afraid of me, but why? She knew I wasn't going to hurt her. I loved her. All I wanted was to show her how much. I wanted to show her that we belonged together, but how could I do that when she was all wrapped up in that nigga. I mean, what the hell did he have that I didn't?

I went to touch her, and she flinched closer to the door. "I'm not gonna hurt you," I said.

"What do you want Lewis? Why are you doing this?" she asked as tears streamed from her eyes.

"What do you mean? You think I came all the way out here to not leave with my girl?"

"I'm not your girl! I have a fiancé! I'm getting married in three weeks!" she cried. The more she talked, the more upset I became.

"The only person you're gonna marry is me! I don't know why you betrayed me like that!"

"Betrayed you? I didn't betray you!"

"Yes, you did! You know that we were together!"

"Lewis, we broke up years ago! This shit that you're doing doesn't make any sense."

"How does it not make sense? I told you when I saw you two weeks ago that I was back in town."

"SO?! What does that mean? Are you telling me that I should've known you were gonna kidnap me?"

"Kidnap you? I don't need to kidnap you, Wynter!"

"But you did! You walked right up to me on the street and kidnapped me at gunpoint!" she said. "The police are probably looking for you right now!"

"Pull out your phone!" I said.

"What?"

"Pull out your phone!"

"I don't have my phone. It's at the party!" she said.

"Then use mine," I said.

"For what?"

"You have to call the police and tell them that I didn't kidnap you. You need to tell them that you left with me

166

because you wanted to," I told her. There was no way I was going to jail for this shit.

"I won't!"

"Yes, you will!"

"NO, I WON'T!!" she said.

"You will or I'll blow your brains out right here, right now!" I threatened.

She wiped her eyes and sat up in her seat. "Then do it!"

"WHAT?!" I asked.

I wasn't expecting her to say that shit. I didn't want to kill Wynter. I really loved her, and I wanted to marry her. I cared about her more than any other woman who had ever been a part of my life. Even Katrina, the girl I thought could replace Wynter. I paid thousands of dollars for Katrina to have plastic surgery so she could look just like Wynter. I should've paid thousands of dollars to sew her pussy shut too because that bitch was cheating on me. After everything I had done to get her to look right, she ended up cheating with the plastic surgeon.

I couldn't believe that shit! I was devastated because I felt as if I had lost Wynter for a second time. Now that I had found her again, how could I just let her marry some other nigga? I couldn't do that. I heard a siren behind me as a police car ordered me to pull over. What the fuck was I being pulled over for?

I looked at Wynter, unsure of what to do. On one hand, I wanted to press the accelerator to the floor and keep it moving. However, if I did that, I knew that they'd come after me with guns blazing. I had to play this shit smart. As the police cruiser continued to follow me with flashing lights and sirens, Wynter looked at me.

"You better pull over," she said.

"I will if you tell them I didn't kidnap you!"

"You did!"

"Don't you understand that if you say that shit, I'm going to jail?!"

"You need to go to jail for what you did! You need help Lewis!" she said.

"Need help for what? For loving you? I don't need help for that. I just need you!"

"Well, I don't need you and if you don't pull over, you're gonna be in even more trouble!"

"Why are you acting like such a bitch? Don't you care about me at all?"

"No Lewis! I don't give a fuck about you! You made the last few months of my senior year miserable. There's nothing you can do that will ever make me wanna get back with you!" Wynter said as she glared at me.

"You sound like you hate me," I said.

The words she had just said were like a knife twisting in my heart. I had never loved a girl the way I loved Wynter. She was the best thing that ever happened to me. How could she not feel about me the way that I did about her? Why was she being so mean to me?

"I don't hate you Lewis, but I definitely do not love you!" she said. "You could hold me hostage for years and I still wouldn't have any love for you!"

Damn! What the fuck was I fighting for then? What the hell was I doing all this for if she would never want me? I had bought a house on the beach for the two of us to live in once we got back from Vegas. I had wanted to give Wynter the world, but she didn't want what I had to offer. I decided to pull over because now there were two police cars following us. I was sure if I kept driving, more would join in the pursuit. As I pulled over to the shoulder, I looked over at Wynter.

"DRIVER, TURN YOUR ENGINE OFF AND STEP OUT OF THE VEHICLE!!"

I turned the engine off. "You can go," I told Wynter.

"You better get out of this car!" she said.

"DRIVER LET ME SEE YOUR HANDS!!"

"Get out of my car Wynter!" I said.

"Oh, trust me, I'm getting out! I truly hope that you get the help that you need," she said.

"You don't need to worry about me. Just go head on and marry your fiancé. Be happy."

"I will."

With that, she slowly opened the door and held her hands up. She stepped out of the car and an officer grabbed her and put her in the rear of the cruiser.

"DRIVER I NEED YOU TO PUT YOUR HANDS OUT THE WINDOW AND STEP OUT OF THE CAR SLOWLY!! DO IT NOW!!"

Wynter didn't want me. She had made that very clear. She didn't even give a shit about me or what happened to me. What the fuck was I even living for? All I ever dreamt about was getting back together with Wynter. Now that I knew there was no hope for us, my life was over. I called my mom because I needed to speak with her.

"Hey baby, how's it going up there?" she asked. Her voice was so cheerful and merry. She was oblivious to the pain that I was experiencing right now.

"Hey mom, it's not going too good. I just wanted to call you and let you know that I love you," I said.

"I love you too baby. Is everything alright? You don't sound like yourself."

"DRIVER THIS IS YOUR LAST CHANCE! SHOW YOUR HANDS AND STEP OUT OF THE VEHICLE SLOWLY!"

"Baby what's going on? What have you gotten yourself into?" she asked as her voice shook with worry.

"Just know that I love you mom. I gotta go," I said and ended the call.

I sent Wynter one last text message. I picked the gun up, put it to my temple and squeezed the trigger.

Chapter eighteen

Zach

Noelle had been blowing up my phone for the past hour. I didn't answer because she had hurt my damn feelings. We had barely spoken since the night of the party. I had seen her reaction when that nigga walked in. The same nigga that had used, abused, and hurt the hell out of her. Yet she sat next to me with her eyes focused on him all night. It was like watching a teenager crushing over some dude.

Then she started crying when he asked his lady to marry him. What the fuck was she crying for? At first I thought she was crying because she wanted me to propose to her. But the more she reacted, the clearer it became. She was crying because she wanted him to propose to her. That hurt was a hard one to swallow. I had done everything in my power to prove to Noelle that she was worthy of love. Not the fake shit that nigga was giving her, but real love.

I wined and dined her. I was there when she needed me. I listened when she talked about her problems and concerns. I exercised with her when she said she was unhappy about her weight. I did everything I could to show her that she deserved more than she had received from him. And what did she do? She showed me what it felt like to fuck myself.

That night I left the party, I tried calling her several times. She didn't answer any of my calls. I sent her numerous text messages, yet she still hadn't responded. I wasn't sure why she was acting that way with me when she knew what kind of dude he was. And the dude had just gotten engaged, so whatever she had hoped for with them should've been done. Right?

Wrong? I didn't hear from Noelle until she finally answered my call three days later. Then she was acting all funny like she didn't wanna speak to me, so I hung up. I hadn't spoken to her since. That's why her phone calls were so surprising to me. I mean, she didn't want to speak to me before, so what changed her mind? Why does she wanna talk now?

I didn't waste any time worrying about it though. The restaurant was pretty busy, and I still had another four hours until I clocked out for the day. I just turned my phone on silent and continued to go about my business. Around 5:50 that afternoon, she walked in. She looked beautiful, but I could tell that there was something different about her. She almost looked like the same girl I fell in love with.

"Hey," she said as she approached me.

"Hey."

"Can we talk?"

"I get off in ten minutes."

"You mind if I wait?"

"If that's what you wanna do," I said and went back to doing what I was doing.

At 6:05, I clocked out and headed to the dining room area. I motioned my head for her to follow me outside. Once outside, I asked, "What are you doing over here?"

"Well, I tried calling you, but you didn't answer. You didn't respond to my texts either, so I came by to check on you," she said.

"I'm good."

"I see that. Why didn't you respond?"

"Because I was busy."

"Too busy for me?" she pouted.

"Too busy for anything outside the restaurant. Besides, I thought you were too busy for me. It ain't like we been communicating this past week," I said.

"I know and I'm sorry about that. I just been busy helping Wynter with the wedding and stuff. Not just that, but she's been having a difficult time since that dude killed himself. I had to be there for her, ya know?"

"Yea, so why are you here now?"

"I missed you Zach. I owe you a huge apology for my behavior this past week. I was such a bitch!"

"Yea, you were."

"Wow!"

"What? Did you think I was just going to say it's okay babe? It wasn't okay. Your behavior was totally uncalled for and unnecessary. If that dude was who you wanted all this time, all you had to do was tell me. Just be honest about yo shit! I would've walked away because I'm nobody's second choice," I said.

"I'm sorry if I made you feel that way. I never meant to hurt your feelings, and you're not my second choice. I guess I just got confused about what I wanted when I saw him propose," she said.

"Oh, so you did want him to propose to you?"

"No, I wanted a proposal from you."

"Huh?" I asked because she had lost me.

"I never thought I could be in a relationship with someone who really loved me the way you do. And knowing how much you love me made me want to get married. I mean, Tripp and Wynter are planning their wedding. Then O'Shea went and proposed. I guess I just got the fever. I'm so sorry for confusing you and making you think that I wanted O'Shea. I just want you Zach. I love you."

She wrapped her arms around my neck and brought her lips to mine. Was she being for real? Was she telling me the truth? I wanted so much to believe her, but I was confused as hell. The way she acted last week told me something totally different.

"Can we go back to my place so I can show you just how sorry I am?" she asked.

"I gotta go home and take a shower first."

"We can take one together," she said as she brought my hand to the front of her dress. As I rubbed against her, I realized she wasn't wearing any panties.

A slow smile crept across my face. "You're so nasty," I said.

"Lemme show you how much."

She kissed me again, this time with some tongue action. It was a good thing we were parked to the side of the building. The customers couldn't see us from the inside, and for that I was grateful. As we finally separated, I walked her to her car. After she slid into the driver's seat, I shut the door. I walked back over to my car and got in. I followed her to her place, anxious to give her what she wanted.

I had missed her just as much as she had missed me. And I was about to show her how much.

Chapter nineteen

Rhianna

Tripp & Wynter's
Wedding Day

I woke up this morning with only one thing on my mind... exposing that bitch for trying to ruin my relationship. I wasn't a petty person by any means, but I was a real one. As long as she stayed in her lane, I was going to stay in mine. But she crossed the line when she came over here without any panties on trying to seduce my man. And when that didn't work, she tried to convince me that the two of them had slept together. What kind of bitch crossed the line that way?

O'Shea and I finally had something real going on and now she wanted to wreck it. She didn't look out for him when he needed someone the most. I was the one that was there for him. He asked me to marry him, so why couldn't she just move the hell on? I guess her man wasn't enough for her, but she couldn't have mine. No way was I about to let her snaky ass ruin our relationship.

The wedding was scheduled for two o'clock this afternoon. I woke up at 10, since I had dragged myself in pretty late last night. Felicia had invited me to attend the bachelorette party with her and I did. I wanted to make that bitch as uncomfortable as I could. However, she didn't seem to care one way or the other. Nor did she approach me to try and apologize. That's what made me believe that she meant for things to go the way that she had hoped.

She thought that she would be successful in getting him back, but she failed. As I made my way to the bathroom to take a shower, I could hear my man snoring in bed. He came in even later than I did following the bachelor party. It was a good thing the wedding was this afternoon, otherwise, the only ones that would be there would be the guests.

I brushed my teeth while the water warmed up in the shower. Then I washed my face with Neutrogena facial wash and rinsed it before climbing in the shower. As I poured liquid soap on the loofa, I heard the shower door slide open. As my man wrapped his arms around me and grabbed my breasts in his hands, I could feel his swollen dick against my back. As he rubbed up against me, I moaned. I was glad that he had found his way into the shower because I could definitely use some loving.

He bent me over before stuffing his burrito into my hot pocket. "Mmmm!" I moaned as he gripped my hips. As he pounded into me from behind, the water rained over us.

It felt so good. Sex in the morning was the absolute best. Well, sex any time of day was alright with me, but morning sex... oh weeeee!

As he continued to pound my pussy out from behind, I relished in the feel of the warm water. After several minutes, our bodies shook almost violently from the orgasms releasing from our bodies. Afterward, I leaned against him as he kissed my neck from behind.

"I love you," I cooed.

"I love you more baby," he said.

We washed each other before rinsing off and climbing out of the shower. As we dried ourselves off, we spoke about how our night was.

"Did you have fun?" I asked.

"Yea, I did. I can't wait to have my own bachelor party," he said.

"Oh yea? So, you want a big wedding?" This was the first conversation about marriage that we had since he proposed. I didn't know that he wanted to have a big wedding. For some reason, I just thought we'd head to Vegas, get married by Elvis and come back home. I never knew he wanted a wedding with family, friends, and expenses.

"I hadn't really thought about it until recently. Hanging with Tripp and doing all this wedding stuff got me feeling some kind of way I guess," he said as he hugged me and kissed the tip of my nose.

"How so?"

"I don't know babe. I guess it's just wedding fever."

"Are you set on having a big wedding or are you open to other options?"

"Like what?" he asked.

"Like a quick wedding in Vegas," I said.

"Why do you want a quick wedding? I thought women liked to have huge ball gowns and big weddings," he said.

"I would just like to be married before the baby gets here."

"What? What baby? Who's having a baby?"

"We are silly," I blushed.

"What? You're pregnant?"

"Yes!"

"How? When?"

"How?"

"Well, not how, but when did you find out?" he asked.

"I just took the test a few days ago. I haven't had it confirmed yet, but I believe it's why I've been so tired lately. And you remember the other morning I threw up. Anyway, I got a test from Walgreen's and it says positive!" I said as I reached in the bathroom drawer and pulled out the test that I had placed in a Ziploc sandwich bag.

I handed the bag to him and he stared at the test. "You're having my baby?" he asked as tears sprung to his eyes. I simply nodded and hugged him tight as my head rested against his chest. He stroked my hair and kissed my forehead as he held me. "I can't believe I'm gonna be a daddy."

"Are you happy? I mean, I know this wasn't planned or anything..."

He grabbed both sides of my face and planted a kiss on my lips. "You have no idea how happy I am. Thank you," he said as he kissed me again.

Shit, now he had me crying. I wondered if it was hormones or something because I knew hormones caused expectant mothers to have mood swings.

"I see we have plans to make concerning our future, but I don't want a Vegas wedding," he said.

"You don't?"

"No, I want my father and our friends to see us say I do. If you want a quick wedding, we can go to city hall and get the justice of the peace to marry us. However, I'd like to get married on the beach. It could be quiet and intimate with just close friends and family. Nothing extravagant like what Tripp and Wynter are doing. You don't have to decide now. You can think about it and we can discuss it at a later time," he said.

"Okay, that's fine. I'm gonna go get dressed and make breakfast. Before you know it, it'll be time to leave."

"I have to leave in less than two hours already, so I'll pass on the breakfast," he said.

"Oh, okay. Well, I'll make breakfast for one."

"Sorry babe. I just have to meet up with Tripp and the other groomsmen at noon. It's already 10:52, so I need to get my shit together. I don't want to forget anything."

"Okay."

"What time are you coming to the hotel?"

"I don't wanna get there too early. I guess around 1:30, so I can find a good seat to take pictures," I said.

"Okay, cool."

So, he went about getting himself together while I headed to the kitchen to find something for me to eat. I decided on oatmeal, sausage and toast. While I was eating, O'Shea was putting stuff in the car. When he was done, he walked over to me and kissed me on the lips.

"I'll see you at the wedding," he said.

"Yep, you sure will. I love you."

"I love you too babe."

Now that I was having his baby, I was more protective of this family than ever. There was nothing I wouldn't do to keep my shit intact. And I mean nothing.

Two and a half hours later, I had parked my car and was walking into the hotel. I headed to the courtyard with only one thing in mind... to find Zach and have a conversation with him. As I walked outside, I was in awe at the beautiful décor and scenery. It was absolutely breathtaking. My eyes did a quick scanning of the room until I spotted who I was looking for. Thank God, he was sitting by himself away from the rest of the guests who were seated and chatting.

I slid in the seat next to him. "Hello," I greeted.

"Hi."

"Do you know who I am?"

He looked over at me. "Not really."

"Well, allow me to properly introduce myself. My name is Rhianna and I'm engaged to O'Shea."

"That part I knew. What can I do for you?" he asked.

"I just wanted to ask you a couple of questions."

"About what?"

"Noelle. Well, you and Noelle... like, where does your relationship stand and all."

"I don't feel the need to discuss my relationship with you. I don't know you," he said.

"Right, I can understand how you would feel that way."

"Good. Then we shouldn't have anything left to say."

"I just wanted to know if your relationship was as solid as you think it is," I said.

"Look, obviously you have some agenda..."

"No, no agenda at all."

"Well, please say what you need to say and go about your business!"

"You don't have to get defensive with me. I'm only trying to help you," I said.

"Help me? Help me do what?"

"Help you to stop making a fool of yourself... well, allowing Noelle to make a fool of you."

"What the hell are you talking about lady?"

"Did you know that two weeks ago Noelle showed up at my fiancé's apartment without any panties and tried to seduce him?" I asked.

"What? You're lying!"

"No, I'm not. She had on a yellow sundress with pink flowers. Oh, and those yellow wedge shoes." I watched as he did a mental checkup. He was probably trying to think about whether he had seen her that day or not. Suddenly, his face took on a different expression. It was one of anger.

"Why are you telling me this?"

"Because I'm pregnant and I can't be stressing about that woman in my life. If y'all are going to be together, you need to keep her in y'all lane. I'm not trying to make trouble for y'all, I promise I'm not. Shit, I want y'all to stay together. But I just thought that you should know what your girl was up to."

With that being said, I got up and moved to another seat. My job was done.

Epilogue

Wynter

I couldn't believe it was finally my wedding day. It couldn't have come at a better time either. I still hadn't told Tripp the good news. I was going to wait to tell him about the baby once we were married. I was totally shocked about the news, but I'm happy, nonetheless. I love Tripp very much and this baby will only bring us closer, if that's possible.

As I stood in the full-length mirror staring at my reflection, I smiled. I was a bride and within the next hour or so, I would be a wife. As my bridesmaids stood around me, I marveled in their appearances. They were so beautiful! What made this day better than ever was the fact that me and my girls had finally found happiness. Brandie and Nelson were planning their wedding, and Zach and Noelle had found their way back to each other. I never thought when we moved to Miami that this was how things would play out.

However, I couldn't be happier.

Brandie

As I stared at my beautiful bestie in her wedding gown, it brought tears to my eyes. She was just so beautiful. I thanked God every day that we were still just as close as we were when we first moved out here to Miami. Things between me and Noelle were strained for a bit, but were better now. I was glad she put all that shit with O'Shea to rest. I would've hated it if she had lost Zach because of that stupid shit.

She deserved a man like Zach in her life. That shit with O'Shea should be a thing of the past. Hopefully, it is now. I was super excited about my relationship with Nelson. He had popped the question a couple of weeks ago and of course, I said yes. I couldn't be happier with the way things have panned out for me and my friends. I was looking forward to what the future held for us.

Tripp

As we made our way down to the courtyard, my nerves kicked in. I wasn't nervous about marrying Wynter. She was the love of my life and I couldn't wait to marry her. I guess I was just nervous because I was getting married. Marriage was a huge step in anyone's life, especially mine since I never thought of getting married until I met Wynter. I was glad that my two best dudes could put their differences aside to be here for me today.

O'Shea and Travis had been on the outs since Travis started a relationship with Tamika, who just happened to be O'Shea's ex. But even though Travis broke the bro code, he was still our brother. Once he got Tamika pregnant, I told O'Shea he had to let that shit go because I knew he didn't want that man to just walk away from his babies. Yea, babies.

As my mom and dad walked me down the aisle, I felt myself tearing up. I didn't want to seem like a weak nigga, but I was happy. As I stood at the altar, I waited anxiously for my girl to appear. Thank you God for all my blessings... especially the one about to meet me at the altar.

O'Shea

Forgiving Travis was something I found difficult to do... at first. When he broke the code, he broke my heart too. We were supposed to be better than that. Tripp helped me see that I had to let go of that hurt. Travis was expecting two babies with his wife. While she was an ex of mine, she was Travis' wife and the mother of his children. Besides, I was engaged to the best woman for me and she was having my baby. I was willing to put all that shit behind us because we were brothers at the end of the day.

As I walked down the aisle with Felicia, I could see how happy Tripp was. I hoped my face shined with just as much happiness right now. I looked at my beautiful fiancée sitting in the second row and I winked at her. I had no idea that Rhianna was the one for me when I was acting the fool with myself. But I know that God doesn't make mistakes. He took me through all that shit to show me how beautiful life could be.

That saying, "God never gives you more than you can handle" is definitely a true statement. Thank God that I have a woman who could be there for me through thick and thin, for better or worse. Oh yea, and Felicia finally forgave me! Life was good.

Travis

My wife was due to have our babies any day now, but she still insisted on being at this wedding to see me walk down the aisle. I was glad that she was here, but I would've preferred her being in bed at home. Tamika and I had been really happy and so blessed. I never knew anyone could make me this happy. I was glad that O'Shea finally came around because I hated the two of us being on the outs, especially now that he had finally got his shit together.

I was really proud of the man he had become. Everyone grows up in their own time. As me and

Brandie prepared to take that walk down the aisle, I smiled. I was so happy for Tripp and Wynter. If anyone deserved this kind of happiness, it was the two of them. It was good to see everyone finally own up to their shit and just grow the hell up. Everything happens for a reason... I truly believed that. I just hoped my wife waited until after the ceremony to go in labor.

Zach

When O'Shea's woman sat beside me, I knew I should've gotten up and left. But I was sitting there first, and if she had something to say, I needed to find out what it was. When she said that Noelle had gone over to O'Shea's to seduce him, I knew that was a lie. But then she described what Noelle had on that day, right down to the fact that she wasn't wearing panties. That was when I remembered exactly what day she was talking about. That was the day that she showed up at the restaurant all apologetic and shit.

When I rubbed up against her and she didn't have any panties on, I thought she had taken them off for me, but that wasn't the case. She had taken them off for O'Shea. Why would she do me like that? I had done nothing but shower her with love, attention and affection. Yet she continued to fuck over me. Well, this was the last straw.

I got up from my seat right before the music began to play for Tripp to walk down the aisle.

I passed him on my way out. He looked at me strangely but didn't say anything. I didn't want him to say anything though, nor did I want him worrying about me on his big day. I left the hotel and sent Noelle a text when I got to the car. I knew it was the coward's way out, but I couldn't even look at her right now if I wanted to. She had played me for a fool, and she had done it for the last fucking time. I already told her that day she came by that I was nobody's second choice and I meant that shit.

I wished her nothing but happiness, but it wasn't going to be with me.

Noelle

Both of my friends were getting married, O'Shea was engaged, Travis was married. Shit, the only thing left was for Zach to propose to me. I wanted that more than anything in this world. Maybe once he saw how beautiful Tripp and Wynter's wedding was and how happy everyone else was, he'd feel the need to propose to me. Thank God I hadn't slept with O'Shea that day. I couldn't even imagine the devastation that mistake would've caused for everyone. I didn't know why I thought I wanted him anyway.

Zach was the man for me. He was the only one who had ever treated me like a queen. He was the only man that had ever told me I was beautiful and meant it when he said he loved me. I would've been a complete fool to have thrown all that away for O'Shea, a nigga that had dogged me and used me more than a hooker used condoms. As I walked down the aisle, I looked for Zach in the seats. I didn't see him at all. I figured I must've missed him, so when I got to the altar, my eyes scanned the entire length of the courtyard for my man. I didn't see him at all.

Where was he? When we texted earlier, he said he was here and couldn't wait to see me. So, where was he now? Maybe he went to the restroom. However, a half hour later, when the ceremony was over, he still hadn't made it to the courtyard. I couldn't wait to get some privacy so I could call him and ask him where he was. But that was going to have to wait because we had a ton of pictures to take, then the walk into the reception ballroom. I finally was able to pull out my phone and call Zach two hours later.

My call went unanswered. I tried calling him several more times, but he still didn't answer. It wasn't until I decided to send a text that I saw that he had sent me a text message. My heart literally dropped to the pit of my stomach when I read it.

Zach: I really thought that you were the one for me, but I was wrong. I can't believe you played me again, but this time was the last time. I hope that you have a happy life, but I need you to know that I won't be a part of it. Please don't call me, text me, or come by my place of business because we have nothing more to say to each other. I told you that day that I wasn't going to be your second choice, and I meant that. You deserve better than the nigga you keep trying to get back with, but for some reason, you can't see that shit. One day, you will know your worth. At least, I hope that for you. Have a nice life Noelle. I wish you all the best.

What the hell happened to change his mind about me? This morning, we woke up in each other's arms and everything was great. What could've happened to ruin what we had worked so hard to build? I rushed to the restroom before anyone could see me crying. I didn't want to ruin Wynter and Tripp's wedding day with my foolishness. My head was spinning, and my heart was aching. This had turned out to be the worst day of my life.

Zach didn't want to speak to me anymore, so how was I going to find out what happened? I called him over and over and over again, but he refused to take my calls. I finally decided to just leave a voicemail.

"Zach, baby I don't know what went wrong, but I need you to answer the phone. I love you Zach and you're not my second choice. You're my first choice, baby. Please pick up the phone so we can work this out. Oh my God! I can't believe this is happening right now! You have to listen to me and believe me when I say I love you," I said as I broke down crying.

If Zach doesn't answer me or call me back, I may never know why he just left me. Then it hit me! I rushed out of the bathroom stall and came face to face with O'Shea's bitch. She was standing against the wall smirking.

"Where's your man?" she asked.

"You did this! You got to him!"

"Yep."

"But why? I thought we were going to leave that shit in the past! Why would you do that?"

"Look, he deserved to know. You don't even love him..."

"YES, I DO! But you ruined it!" I wanted to slap the shit out of her, but what good would that do? It still wouldn't get Zach to take me back. It still wouldn't change the fact that she and O'Shea were getting married.

Slapping her wouldn't do shit but make me as ghetto as she was. I wasn't going to stoop to her level, not on my best friend's wedding day. Maybe tomorrow, I'd whoop her ass, but not today. Today was Wynter's day, so no matter how bad I was hurting or how bad I wanted to hurt her, I had to keep my cool.

"If today wasn't my bestie's wedding day, I'd mop the floor with your ghetto ass! Next time I see you, you may not be so lucky," I threatened.

"Uhm, that's probably going to have to be put on hold for about eight months. At least until after I give birth. Then if you still wanna hook up, I'm there. I just want you to leave my man alone," she said.

I couldn't get over the fact that she was pregnant. She ruined my life for what? What was the purpose of her doing what she did? "Why did you tell him?"

"He deserved to know."

"That wasn't your place."

"I made it my place. It wasn't your place to try and seduce my fiancé, but you did it anyway."

"Well, he left me. Are you happy now? Was that what you wanted?" I asked.

"Not really. I just thought he should know."

"You're an evil bitch! I sure hope O'Shea knows how evil you are," I said.

"Shit, he should know since he trained me so well," she laughed. "Enjoy the rest of your night."

With that, she walked out the door. As much as I wanted to grab her by the hair, I restrained myself from doing that. She wasn't to blame for Zach leaving me. This was my doing. If I had never shown up at O'Shea's house, this would've never been an issue. I had to own up to my mistake and face the consequences of my actions...something people often didn't do.

One day, I'd find the right man for me at the right time. It just wasn't my time. I looked at myself in the mirror. I had to make sure I looked presentable to go back out and join the party. Nothing was going to ruin my friend's wedding day, especially not me.

The end!